D1594275

IN TIME FOR AN AMISH CHRISTMAS

AMISH CHRISTMAS BOOKS: BOOK 1

SAMANTHA PRICE

CHAPTER 1

Sunday, December 17

"I DON'T THINK it's fair what you're doing."

Heidi studied Janelle's stony face as they sat at the bar with their seats half-turned toward one another. Janelle's pinched lips were proof that encouraging her best friend to work for her might not have been the greatest idea she'd ever had. It was important that Janelle be empathetic to the other realtors in the firm. After all, they were a team. Heidi chose her words carefully. "That's the thing, though, I'm trying to be fair to everyone. They say I'm giving you the best leads."

"That's only because I'm the best closer and can get the job done." Janelle pouted her glossy red-painted lips and looked away.

Heidi admired red lips on Janelle. She was the only person Heidi knew who looked good in lipstick that color.

True-red lipstick wouldn't suit for herself, anyway, not with all the red tones in her brown hair. Her own Amish upbringing hampered her in regard to wearing too much makeup or picking bright shades. Even though she'd left the Amish years ago, some of the basic principles were still stuck within her heart.

Janelle wasn't finished with her rant, and with a toss of her head she turned back to face Heidi. "Give them the lower-priced properties and it won't matter if they lose them. When they get better, then that'll be a different story."

Heidi had put a lot of effort into training Janelle and in the past two years her friend's closing rates had been second only to her own. Before she'd come to work for Heidi, Janelle had sold blinds and awnings. When Janelle found out how much money she could make in real estate, Heidi didn't have to ask her twice to get her realtor's license and come work for her in her start-up business.

"They know how many deals you close, but they said they weren't being given the same chance...and they've got a point." The other realtors in the company weren't happy with getting leftovers, and Heidi didn't want to lose any of them to her competitors because they were all above average and would become better with more training and experience.

Janelle shook her head slightly and twitched her lips into a quick frown, showing her displeasure in the topic of conversation.

"I've come up with an idea. I'm thinking of grading the agents into tiers—different levels. Levels one, two, and three. You'll obviously be level one based on your results, so you'll get the higher-priced —"

"No."

Heidi was shocked at her friend being so adamant. She'd grown far more confident since she married Scott six months ago. Right now, Heidi wasn't sure if that was a good thing. "But wait; you haven't even heard —"

Janelle leaned closer. "Why can't we leave things as they are? If you start giving them more leads they might lose them. Skye told me Tyrone didn't even show at an appointment yesterday and she had to send Jennique to cover for him."

Heidi put her head in her hands. It was hard to keep twelve agents, four assistants and two receptionists happy. If one person was happy, it was a certainty that others weren't. Until the place was ticking along nicely, she could kiss the idea of opening more offices goodbye. She took a sip of her gin and tonic. She didn't normally drink, another outcome of being raised by non-drinking Amish parents, but she told herself her staff were driving her to it.

"Anyway," Janelle said, "let's talk about the Christmas party. Are we still having it on the twenty second?"

"Let's finish talking about this first. We've got a problem here and we need to find a way to fix it."

"I don't have the problem, you do."

Heidi was a little shocked. "Yes, and right now *you're* at the heart of the problem."

Janelle giggled. "All right, tell me what you're thinking."

Heidi sighed, and then gave her friend a wry smile.

"I've got a few ideas. I'll solidify them, put them on paper and then we'll talk again. How's that?"

"Sounds like a plan. Now, what is your answer about the Christmas party?"

"It's all arranged and we're having it on the twenty-second, and it's at the office, same as always."

Janelle took off talking about the Christmas party with a whole different attitude. It seemed everyone was excited about Christmas. Everyone except for Heidi. Heidi stared into her drink and stirred the ice with the thin black straw. She'd loved Christmas when she was a child, but having no one to share it with, it had lost its meaning. Christmas Day had been such fun back then. Her child-hood home would be full of people, gifts, and delicious foods her mother had prepared. The walls and windows were decorated with paper lanterns and candles sat on the windowsills. She and her mother always began preparing for Christmas weeks before. Often at night, while gentle snow fell, she and her parents would huddle by the fire talking and laughing about their day.

"Are we using the same caterer as last year?" Janelle asked.

"Yes, I've already booked them. It's all under control." Everyone who worked for her had a significant other except for Tyrone, who had a different girl every week. Heidi hated always going to functions alone, especially the Christmas ones.

"Are you going back home for Christmas again this year?"

"Someone's got to stay and work." When Heidi saw her

friend opening her mouth about to protest, she quickly added, "Yes. I'm going back briefly. Don't worry." At eighteen, Heidi had chosen to go on *rumspringa,* chasing her dream of going to New York to become a model. She'd had a desperate need to wear makeup and fancy clothes. Sadly, things didn't go according to plan and she was rejected by every modelling agency because she was too short. As a matter of survival, she got a job as an assistant for a realtor. After she saw how much money the realtors made, she convinced her boss to take her on as an associate and got herself licensed. After a couple of years in sales, she recognized an opportunity in the leasing market and opened her own agency specializing in rentals only.

"You really shouldn't work so hard."

"I have to." Heidi had been determined to get to the top and have her photo on the cover of Forbes magazine. Maybe even become one of the wealthiest realtors in the world. Her plan was to expand, to open more offices. But first she had to get her agency working like a well-oiled machine, and with all the squabbles and infighting, it was anything but. She needed a way to foster an atmosphere of healthy competition amongst her staff.

"You should stop and smell the roses, like I do."

"I do that, too."

"No, you don't!"

"I have slowed down since I don't do the appointments anymore." Apart from training staff, she sought out new opportunities and new directions for the business to take. Most of her days were long, which left little time for a social life and that was just as well because she had no

SAMANTHA PRICE

one with whom to socialize. Her 'friends' were business acquaintances.

"Scott said he's got a friend who'd suit you. He's a retired baseball player."

"No thanks." Heidi rolled her eyes and fiddled with her new short spiky hair. She knew his type—the retired athlete. Besides that, everyone Janelle and her boyfriend, well, her husband now, had suggested in the past had been totally unsuitable.

"Don't be like that. He's different from the others."

"I've given up on dating. Although, having said that, if I meet a wonderful man I won't send him away."

"Glad to hear it." Janelle's eyes twinkled with a hint of mischief.

That told Heidi Janelle might be up to something such as causing her to 'accidentally' bump into someone. She had to get that idea out of her friend's head. "I want to be in a relationship with someone special, but I don't like the type of man I've been meeting lately. Their egos are way too big. Anyway, don't worry about me. I'm fine." She sucked in a last swallow of her gin and tonic through the straw.

"You're not fine if you're going to spend another Christmas by yourself."

"I won't be by myself. I just said—"

"And who are you going to be with?"

"I said I'm going home, same as I go home every year."

"What, for a day?" Janelle asked.

"That'll be enough, believe me. I don't belong there anymore, so a day and a night is more than enough."

"I don't know what ever happened between you and

6

your family. All I know is that you're an only child and I'm guessing your family weren't well-to-do because you arrived here with nothing." Janelle's blue eyes opened wide. "Or, are they wealthy and they cut you off without a cent? What did you do?"

Heidi blew out a deep breath. "You've got such an imagination."

"I have to use my imagination because you never tell me anything."

Heidi jiggled her straw amongst the ice causing it to make a tinkling sound against the glass. "There's not much to tell. Anyway, I'm thinking of getting a cat."

"Then you'll become a mad cat lady."

"Mad?" Heidi rolled her eyes. "Thanks."

"Well, not mad, but you know what I mean. Do you really want to become a cliché?"

"There's nothing wrong with cats. I can't get a dog because I've got no time to walk it. Dogs need too much attention."

"And you don't have any time to properly look after a cat. Why don't you get a goldfish if you want a pet?"

"No way! I'd have to clean out the tank, yuck, and where would I find the time to do that?"

Janelle laughed. "You can always pay someone to walk the dog, and to clean the fish tank, or bowl, or whatever fish are kept in."

"That's true. I could."

Janelle looked at her watch. "Are we nearly finished? I promised to meet Scott to do some Christmas shopping."

"We haven't finished what we've come here to talk about, but we've made a start. I guess you can go."

Janelle got off her stool, took hold of her black Chanel purse, and said, "You can't give those losers any good leads. They won't close them, and we'll both end up losing money. It'll affect your money too."

"They don't close as many as you, but they're quite good. They aren't losers. You know I don't take in losers."

The staff were on commission-based wages and that created Heidi's problem; if she didn't start giving them good leads, they'd leave. The worst thing for a business was a continual turnover of staff. "I've been thinking of a few options to keep everyone happy. One of the things I've been chewing over is easing you into more of a training role. You'll spend part of your time training and you'll get a cut of what they make. I'll take it out of the company's cut so no one loses out. How does that sound?"

Janelle sat back down. "Now you're talking my language."

"I'll come up with a few scenarios and a payment scale and then we'll talk again. You go off and keep Scott happy. I don't want to stand in the way of love." Heidi giggled.

Janelle smiled, leaned over and kissed Heidi on her cheek. "Thanks, you're the best."

After Janelle left, Heidi sat there at the bar alone and, totally out of character, ordered another drink.

As it often did, her mind wandered to the man she had left behind when she'd left her Amish community—Derek Miller. They'd been dating for six months and she was sure he'd follow when she left. He'd talked about going on *rumspringa,* too, and then decided against it. He was upset she wanted to be a model; she was certain that made him change his mind about her. She tried to convince him it wasn't what he thought. She wasn't going to be a Playboy centerfold, or show off too much skin. All she wanted was to walk the catwalk and feel like a real woman, to get to dress up in nice clothes and makeup.

She sipped her drink and once again wondered what would've happened between her and Derek if she'd stayed. It wasn't until some years later and dozens of bad first dates that she appreciated the rare love they had shared. It was hard to find a good and caring man who was also faithful and loving. The men she'd dated in the past few years only cared about themselves. Derek had always put her first. She sighed. There was no use thinking about him now. The time for them had passed. He was probably married by now, to a devoted wife and with a herd of children, and that was why she tried to avoid thoughts of him and what might have been.

"Can I buy you a drink?"

Heidi was jolted out of thinking about Derek. She looked over at the man who'd just sat next to her. Going by his slurred speech and his rumpled blue suit, she made a good guess that he'd been drinking all day. "No, thank you. I was just going."

"Stay a while. Have another drink." He stared at her. "You've got the most glorious blue eyes and they go so well with your red hair. Is it natural?"

"My eyes?"

He chuckled. "Your hair." She frowned at his attempt at flirtation, and when she didn't answer, he picked up her glass and looked at it. "What are you drinking?"

"Nothing." She wasn't going to sit there and drink alongside him, especially not after having had two drinks already, something she almost never did. She stood up, grabbed her purse and pulled her coat off the back of the chair and went to walk away.

"Wait." He reached for her arm and she moved it away just in time. "You're beautiful. Are you a model?"

"No. I'm too short." She turned and walked out of the bar ignoring the man's protests. She knew she wasn't as attractive as she once was. The man probably didn't think she was as beautiful as he'd said, and he was obviously too drunk to see properly.

The biting cold wind assaulted Heidi's cheeks as soon as she stepped into the night air, thankful her home was only a few blocks away. She pulled on her coat as she walked and once she had it on she pulled out a beanie and rammed it down over her head to cover her ears, regretting the newly cut hair that left them exposed to the biting cold. Even after so many years away from the community, having her hair cut this short had made her feel a small amount of guilt. After all, a woman's hair was her crowning glory according to the bible. Amish women were never supposed to cut their hair.

Heidi put her head down and walked faster, all the while thinking about her old boyfriend, Derek Miller. Every time she was lonely or sad, her mind drifted to him. It was unfair that to choose him she would've also had to stay in the community closeted from the outside world. She couldn't fathom living without the movies she watched late at night to wind down, or the fast food she lived on, or the Internet. There was more to life than making babies, cooking, washing, sewing, and attending church social gatherings. Besides, Derek had allowed her to walk right out of his life. If he'd really loved her, he would've found her and begged her to return.

A sudden gust of wind splattered large droplets of icy rain against her face. She looked up at the sky to a blinding flash of lightning. She jumped as its large clap of answering thunder sounded, rumbling across the darkness. Then the rain started pelting down on the road alongside her. Hurrying to get to the warm haven of her apartment, she stepped onto the road and heard screeching brakes. She jumped out of the way just in time. The car blasted its horn and drove off fast as Heidi pressed her hand to her thundering heart. She could've died right there in the street.

WHEN HER APARTMENT building came into view, she saw Dennis, the temporary doorman. That meant Stuart was sick again. She'd been caught up talking to Dennis twice and both times she couldn't get away for close to half an hour. To avoid him talking to her again, she pulled out her phone and pretended someone was on the other end of the line. Hopefully, that would deter Dennis from launching into a long and tedious conversation about his damp basement that his landlord refused to fix.

As she approached the building with her phone to her ear, Dennis didn't look happy, but he pulled the door open for her and stepped aside. She gave him a little nod, thanked him and kept walking. Then she continued swiftly into the elevator. Behind the safety of the closed doors, she put her phone away.

In minutes, she was on the second floor and in her

apartment. Her home was her sanctuary and a direct reflection of her success. Since she'd bought it a year ago, she had redesigned the kitchen and the two bathrooms. The bathrooms were all white Carrara marble with black fittings and tapware. The kitchen carried on the same black and white theme, with a touch of steel. There was nothing out of place and nothing that didn't need to be there. It was as far away as she could get from an Amish home and that's exactly how she'd wanted it.

She took off her hat and coat and left them hanging to dry in the open closet by the door. She headed out to the living room and slumped onto the couch. Off came her shoes, and she picked up the TV remote, hit the power button and flicked through the channels. A good show was what she needed to cheer herself up. It was hard having no one to share the good times with, and harder still, having no one to share the bad times. She never thought she'd be alone forever, but with every passing day it was becoming a stronger possibility.

It wasn't unusual for her to think about Derek at this time of year. For the first couple of years, she'd waited for him to knock on her door, but she soon came to terms with the fact that he wasn't coming after her and he'd gotten married to some lucky woman. Going without love was a sacrifice she had to make to reach her goals.

She threw the remote down on the coffee table in frustration. There was never anything good on TV at Christmastime and especially not on a Sunday. The Christmas specials were either too childish or too sappy. She reminded herself to get pay TV. *That's something I'll do in the new year*, she thought. All the serials and reality TV shows she enjoyed had finished. And that left only reruns of movies she'd already seen.

After she had put one of her frozen dinners in the microwave to heat, she headed to her room to fetch the one thing that would make her feel closer to Derek and her old community, if she could find it. She rummaged through her drawers in her expansive walk-in-closet until she recalled she'd seen it on the top shelf of the linen closet in the hallway.

She opened the door of the closet and couldn't reach the top shelf without standing on a chair. After she dragged a chair from the dining room, she reached up and her hand touched something that could've been it. She grabbed the edge of it and pulled. *Yes.* There it was. Her grandmother's diary that her father had given her the day she left the community.

Tucking it under her arm, she lifted the chair and used one foot to nudge the door of the linen closet shut. She took the chair back to the dining room and set the book in the living room. She went into her bedroom and changed into comfy clothes and then curled up on the living room couch to reminisce.

In all the time she'd had it, she'd only leafed through it once or twice. There were recipes every three or four pages, but mainly it was a travelogue of all the places Agnes, her grandmother, had visited before she married. Every time she'd looked at the book, she had marveled at her grandmother's handwriting. It revealed what an exacting and meticulous person she had been.

When the microwave beeped, Heidi closed the book

SAMANTHA PRICE

and left it on the coffee table while she ate her dinner in the kitchen.

After her dinner of roasted lamb and vegetables, she had another surf through the TV channels. There was still nothing worth watching. She leaned over and grabbed her grandmother's book and started to read her recipes along with the handy hints. The recipes were written in such a way that it made Heidi feel she could follow them and they would turn out okay. That hadn't been the case in the past when she'd followed other people's recipes. After a little more reading, she took the book to bed, deciding to read the diary from the beginning.

CHAPTER 2

CAREFUL OF THE yellowed pages of her grandmother's diary, Heidi started at the beginning.

This diary belongs to Agnes Hostetler. I am a woman of twenty years and have started on a most exciting journey. My life begins today. I have decided to write my life experiences and no longer will I be an onlooker, I will be a partaker of life. This day marks day one of my six-week journey that my parents have designed for me. I will be visiting relations and friends of my mother, who are scattered all over the country. I don't know who I'm writing this for, but a journey such as this surely needs to be accompanied by a written record.

I am the youngest of three sisters and we have two older brothers. All are in the Amish faith, and all are married except for my sister Amy, and myself. Amy is engaged to be married to Harold in three months' time. Why have my parents (John and Greta) decided to send me away? They said it was something that was for my own good. I've known about it for two weeks, since I overheard them talking about it. I was going to bed one night and walked past their door and heard my name mentioned. I was curious and stopped still to listen.

"We have spoiled her," I heard my father say. "Not only because she was the youngest, but she was smaller than the others and didn't feed as well. We carried on being overly protective. We let fear into our hearts instead of trusting God. He gave her to us, and He will look after her on this journey you intend to send her on."

"We have spoiled her. It's true, jah," my mother agreed. "She's taken an almost arrogant approach and questions everything. She is not at all like the others, who were so obedient and took our advice about choosing good husbands and fraas. She has not been made to do chores like the others and she has never seen hardship."

I was hurt and shocked at what they'd said. For so long I'd begged Mamm and Amy to let me help in the kitchen and each time they sent me off. It's no wonder I lost interest with so much rejection. It's not my fault, it's theirs.

Dat said, "She has developed into a dreamer. Her mind is not on the earth, it is in the clouds somewhere."

"Jah, and she's not even interested in cooking and cleaning like other maidels. She takes no thought of choosing a husband and I despair of what will become of her when we go home to Gott."

"I know."

"I will miss her, but I see no other way."

My vadder said, "Nee. That's true. Surely you know it is just as hard on me to part with her for six weeks as it is for you."

"Jah, dear, I know it is hard for you."

"So, dry those tears. She will have to help with lots of chores in every place we send her."

"I have written to them all and let them know what must be achieved from her visits. I know everyone will help. And, I have that special plan we talked about."

"Special plan?" They were sending me away. What plan? I was pleased they were upset about me being away, at least. From then on, I could hear no more as their voices became muffled. I was upset they thought this way about me. I was born early, weeks before I was supposed to be, and I nearly died. It was true I wouldn't feed properly as a baby, and now they think I'm spoiled.

After hearing this conversation between my parents, I hurried to my own room. I was filled to overflowing with excitement that they were sending me off to travel. That's something I'd always wanted to do from the time I was a little girl. At that moment, I thought to buy a blank book, so I could write down everything I would learn in those six weeks.

My parents think I can't do anything and they despair of me. I will show them I can do everything better than everyone else, but I have not been given the chance or, sometimes, I've just chosen not to, up to now.

I will learn to be the best cook; I will collect recipes and learn to be an expert at running a household. I will be so good that I will be even better than their expectations.

If I marry, I will find a husband that suits me and the love won't be swooning. It will be a practical kind of love. I will find a good man. If they think I'm a dreamer, they are in for a big shock.

That's what I decided that night after I heard my parents' plan.

Now, I am writing this on the bus to my first destination, in a book I'm going to use to record everything that happens. I bought the book at the mercantile store. The bus is quieter than I thought it would be and it trembles. This is the first time I've been on one. The scenery is passing so fast before my eyes. It's much faster than a buggy; it almost makes me dizzy at times. There are beautiful pastures with valleys and hills in the distance. My thoughts go back to my parents' conversation about the plans they hold for me.

There was one part of it I could not understand. The part where my mother said she had a secret plan. What could it be?

AFTER HALF AN HOUR of reading about Agnes's adventures, Heidi's eyes closed and she could feel herself fading. She shut the book, and held it to her chest while her thoughts turned again to Derek Miller. Tears flooded down her cheeks. Why had she been so stupid as to leave him? All the money in the world couldn't buy the love they'd had. With him, she'd had everything she'd ever wanted and yet she went in search of something else. Heidi had always prided herself on being a smart woman, but now she knew she wasn't.

Heidi wanted to be more like Agnes, who took enjoyment in simple things. Most of the Amish did that, and that was something she missed about her Amish kinfolk. Agnes wouldn't have left God and the only man she'd ever loved to chase riches and silly notions. At that moment, Heidi judged her whole life as a waste. It had been vanity when she'd had the idea of being a model, wanting others to admire her prancing around like a fool on a catwalk. It was pride to amass a fortune just so others would think well of her business acumen, and she had wanted people to be surprised that she, a mere woman, could achieve so much.

In that moment, she realized she was working so hard just so that others would think well of her. When all was said and done and her life was over, what would she have accomplished? It was a comfort that she had been able to provide jobs for her workers and be of good service to her clients, but she was more than her job. She needed more. Was it too much to ask for a male companion? It seemed everyone she knew had one without even trying.

Gott, *what have I done? I abandoned you without a second thought, chasing vanity and pride. I also left Derek in the same way. What can I do to right the wrongs I've made? Help me turn my heart back to you. Please find me a man and some worthy purpose to my life.*

She knew it was too late to fix her mistakes, and she cried lonely tears until she was exhausted. Then she got out of bed and splashed her face with cold water, returned to bed and picked up the diary again to read more. Often reading helped her to fall asleep.

WHAT PLAN DOES my mother have? The way she talked about it, it sounded like another plan or another part of the plan and not just the journey. What is my mother up to? I will find that out soon enough. She is quite sly, but not in a bad way. Not like a fox that lies in wait to kill the chickens, taking the smallest or the weakest, or the one on its own. She is sly in the way that she works things out, and is always thinking, planning, and plotting things. I wonder if all mothers are like that.

I was happy my parents told me they would miss me as I was leaving. I know they think they're doing the best thing for me and they're not just sending me away to have some peace and quiet for themselves.

I already miss Furball, my darling cat. He sleeps all day on my bed, and all night too. I've rarely seen him outside of the house in these last years. He loves to be stroked and patted. In the daytime, he gets under my quilt and looks like a lump on my bed. Still, I love him and he keeps me company. I found him near a bakery when I was a young girl. I saw him by himself and he was only a kitten. I screamed for Dat *to stop the buggy, and when* Mamm *found out why I wanted to stop she said no and I got into big trouble for screaming.*

Dat *stopped the buggy anyway. It was the first time and the only time I remember that he went against what* Mamm *said. He was the one who got out of the buggy and got the little kitty. My mother and I watched from the buggy as he crouched down and coaxed the kitty to come to him. He picked him up, put him under his coat, and carried him back to us.*

When Dat *got back to the buggy, he handed him to me. He looked scared and dug his claws into me.* Dat *took off his coat and wrapped him in it and then the kitty was fine.*

I held the wrapped-up kitty all the way home, and Mamm *was cranky all the way home and she said he'd grow into a furball. I had no idea what she meant but I didn't care. I knew I'd be allowed to keep him. Anyway, that's how Furball got his name.*

I think Dat *wanted him just as much as I did, and then by the time we got home, he had talked* Mamm *into me keeping him. She said we had barn cats and we had more than enough.* Dat *said, if we didn't give him a home he would come to a bad end. Eventually,* Mamm *came around.*

Now, the bus has just come to a stop. I must ask if this is where I'm supposed to get off. More later.

Now it is night time as I write this.

After I got off at Holmes County, I saw my Auntie Elsie waving to me. She looks like an older version of my mother. Onkel Robert *followed her as they walked fast to meet me.*

The buggy ride to their farm was full of surprises. Instead of flat paddocks and pastures like I was used to seeing, the country-side was hilly with small lumpy bushes rather than tall trees. When we turned a corner sharply, I saw the house in front of me. It was built on a hill, little more than a cabin.

I counted twenty steps leading up the hill and to the front door. Once I reached the porch and looked back, I could see why they'd built the house there. They could see their entire property. It was a beautiful scene.

I was left to have a little rest before I met my cousins. I had not met them before because of the long distance between us. I'd met my aunt and onkel *a couple of years before when they came to a wedding by themselves.*

A little later, I met the cousins. Sally Anne is my age, Margaret two years older, then there's Aaron and his twin, Miriam, who are one year older again. Titus is the oldest and he's very handsome. He's married, but staying here to help my onkel *increase the water supply to the farm.*

These are the conversations that were had today as clear as I can remember them.

"Dinner will be ready in one hour, Agnes. You have had a long trip. Have a rest and Sally Anne will call you when dinner's ready."

"Denke, Aunt Elsie."

Later, sitting at the dinner table, Aunt Elsie said, "Have some of this lovely stew. Sally Anne prepared it while we were collecting you from the train. It is my Mammi's *chicken and onion stew. All the ingredients come from the farm here."*

I had a mouthful and declared it was more than delicious and asked Aunt Elsie if I could have the recipe and be shown how to make it. She said that she would show me before I left.

Now, this is what shocked me:

In front of everyone, Sally Anne said, "We were told you were lazy and very spoiled, and you think cooking and sewing are not for you."

Aunt Elsie said, "Stop it, Sally Anne. You were not told anything of the kind."

"Well, you left the letter from Aunt Greta lying around, and I read it."

"You are very rude to read my mail, and to say such a thing at the table." Aunt Elsie shook her head and couldn't look at me.

"She might be rude, Auntie, but she's honest," I said, "I was like Sally Anne just said, probably still am, but I want to change. Will you all help me? I want to learn to cook and sew and to collect some of your recipes, Aunt Elsie, and to help a lot on this lovely farm." I looked around the table and gave everyone what I hoped was a sincere smile. I was determined to beat everyone at their own game, and improve myself at the same time. I showed Sally Anne I wasn't embarrassed by what she said.

Now it is the next night and dinner was pork casserole with sauerkraut. From the little things she says and does, Sally Anne has made it clear that she doesn't like me and she goes out of her way to show it. I will write more about that tomorrow.

So I don't lose them on a scrap of paper, I'm writing the recipes I've learned so far in my book.

Mammi's Chicken and Onion stew.
Ingredients

2-4 tablespoons of cooking oil or fat
1 whole chicken (about 5#) cut into pieces
1-2 pounds onions, thin-sliced
1 pound carrots, sliced or chopped
1 pound peas-in-pods, whole or halved
2-5 cloves of garlic, minced
salt and pepper to taste
Herbs as desired (sage, thyme, rosemary, marjoram ...)
Chives or parsley for garnish, snipped

Cookware
Large soup pot
Large frying pan

Method:
In frying pan, brown chicken pieces in 2 tablespoons
of oil.
Transfer to soup pot and cover with water, rinsing juices
from frying pan into soup pot. Cover the pot.
Bring to a boil, then simmer for 1 to 2 hours. (If desired,
debone the chicken at this point, and return meat to soup
pot) continue to simmer.

In frying pan, brown sliced onions in 1 – 2 tablespoons of
oil or fat. Then add 1 cup water and stir. Add onions and
broth to the soup pot, and continue to simmer.
Add carrots, garlic, and choice of herbs, and simmer until
carrots are tender.
Add peapods, simmer 10 – 20 min.
Salt and pepper to taste.
Thicken with flour or roux.

*Add water as needed during cooking time to make desired amount of gravy.

*Serve with boiled red-skin potatoes or with mashed potatoes.

*Makes a good soup, too, with added liquid and seasonings to make more broth, and any other added vegetables you choose.

Pork Casserole with Sauerkraut

Ingredients:

5 pounds pork ribs with meat

1 pound onions, sliced thin

2 – 4 quarts sauerkraut, amount based on your preferences

1-2 tablespoons black peppercorns

2 tablespoons cooking oil or fat

Cookware:

1 or 2 large and deep casserole dishes with lids

Large frying pan

Method:

Heat oven to 375° F

In frying pan, brown onions in cooking oil or fat.

Layer in bottom of casserole dish (dishes) including liquid from pan.

Place ribs in a layer over onions.

Sprinkle with peppercorns.

Spread sauerkraut over top of meat, adding juice as well.

Add 1 – 2 cups water, then cover with lid.

Bake in hot oven (375° F) for 1 – 2 hours, until bubbling around sides of casserole dish.

Lower oven temperature to 250° F and bake for several more hours.

Add water if needed to prevent drying out.

Done when meat is 'fall-apart-tender.'

Usually does not need added salt, but put some on the table for individual use.

Serve with mashed potatoes and garden vegetables of choice.

CHAPTER 3

Monday, December 18

"Wake up, Heidi."

A male voice? She must be dreaming. Before she dared open her eyes, she tried to remember the night before. She'd gone to sleep in her own bed, she was absolutely certain of it. Slowly, she opened her eyes and saw a fuzzy figure looming over her. She froze, too scared to scream and then she realized that the man was Derek.

"Derek," she heard herself say as she looked into his hazel eyes.

"Heidi," he said again.

"Yes, it's me." She was dreaming! She grabbed hold of his hand and he put his arms around her.

"You're okay now," he whispered.

"I thought I'd never see you again."

He moved back and then picked up her hand and held it tight. "Are you all right?"

"I don't know." It was then she realized she wasn't in her own room. *Of course not. How would he have gotten inside?* She saw boards running horizontally across the wall, and the furnishings told her she was in a farm house. "Where am I?"

"You're at home. I couldn't wake you."

She stared at Derek's beautiful face. He was older, his build was heavier, and his features were more manly than boyish. Her dream sure was lifelike. She looked around the room again. "Where are we?"

He leaned over and stroked her hair. "At home. It's all right, I'll stay home with you today. Your *Mamm's* been here and taken the girls for the day. We'll fetch them later."

"Who?"

He frowned looking almost sympathetic. "I'll bring some breakfast up to you before Michael wakes."

She couldn't speak. *Who is Michael? Who are 'the girls?'* Derek was wearing his usual Amish clothes. She looked down at their hands linked together. Since she could feel his touch, it seemed real and not like a dream. "Where am I? What's happened?"

"You fell down the porch steps yesterday when you were trying to get the girls out of the rain. Don't you remember?"

"No. What girls?"

"Are you joking? Because you're scaring me right now."

She dropped his hand and scooted further to the edge of the bed. This was real. It was no dream.

He straightened up and rubbed an eyebrow. "You had a fall last night." He ran a hand through his nearly-shoulder-length dark hair. "I should've sent for the doctor then and there."

"Not the doctor."

"Yes, the doctor. I'm sorry, Heidi, but I'm worried. If you're still like this in an hour or two, I'm going to have to get the doctor. I'll go heat up Michael's bottle."

She opened her mouth to speak, but he was already out of the room. Then she looked over toward the window and saw a crib. She got out of bed realizing she was in a cotton Amish-style nightgown, but she was more concerned about who was in the crib. Lying there wrapped in a white shawl was a small baby who couldn't have been more than six-months-old. She got a fright when long hair fell across her face. Then she touched her hair and it was long again—not at all the short-cropped hair she'd had when she had fallen asleep.

The baby making snuffle noises drew her attention away from her hair. She looked in the crib again and when she saw he was okay, she swung around. In an effort to make sense of what was happening, she flung open the doors of the closet. There were women's Amish dresses, boots and shoes, and with a closer look, the shoes were all in her size. In the adjoining closet were men's clothing.

Next, she looked through the chest of drawers. In the bottom drawer was paperwork. She pulled out a handful and leafed through the pages. The biggest piece of paper was a marriage certificate. Scanning the names, she saw her name and Derek's—she was married to Derek. It was dated a month after she'd left the Amish community.

Needing to sit, she headed back to the bed, still staring at the marriage certificate. Then she remembered how she'd cried out to God when she had cried herself to sleep the night before ... when she was in her own bed in her own apartment. Had God answered her prayers in a weird and wonderful way, or was she just having a weird dream? Maybe God was giving her a vision to show her what she'd missed out on by leaving the community.

Her gaze traveled to the baby in the crib by the window. He'd never have come into this world because she had never married Derek.

"This is what people mean by their life flashing before them before they die," she said softly. "Except, this is the life I would've had if I'd never left the community."

Derek walked back into the room. "Here you go." She looked up to see him with a mug in his hands. "What are you doing with that?" He nodded toward the marriage certificate.

"I don't know. Just looking at it."

"Here's your coffee." He placed it down on her night-stand. "I'll go cook your eggs just as you like them—not runny."

"Thanks. I'm rather hungry."

"You're what?"

"Hungry."

"*Gut.* You'll feel better once you eat."

"Maybe I will." Whatever was happening, she'd play along until she figured it out. "The girls are at *Mamm's* you said?" She wondered how old they were, and were they hers and Derek's? They couldn't have been *that* old, and just how many of them were there?

"*Jah*, that's right."

She drank a mouthful of coffee. "This is good."

"*Denke*." He chuckled. "You don't normally allow me in the kitchen. I'm looking forward to making your eggs."

She looked up at him, still thinking about the coffee. "It's ground coffee and not instant."

He frowned at her. "That's right."

"I don't let you in the kitchen?" She lowered the hot mug into her lap. She wasn't doing a great job of going along with what was happening, not with that stupid question.

"*Jah*, the kitchen's your domain, you always tell me."

Heidi laughed. She found it odd that he said that. She hated cooking and never cooked anymore, not since she'd found the excellent people who delivered the home-cooked freezable meals. All she had to do was pop them in the microwave. She took her mind off food and coffee, and stared back down at the marriage certificate.

He said, "Have you lost your memory?"

She stared at him. She'd touched him and she had felt him, and everything seemed so clear. Normally, her dreams weren't like that. "Am I dreaming?"

"You think you're having a dream?"

"I am having a dream, and you're not real."

"Aha. Why do you think you're dreaming?"

"That's just it, it's not my real life. I never got a chance to … *Gott* is giving me this chance to see you again. I've always thought about you over the years."

"You're not dreaming, and I have no idea what you're

talking about. You fell and you hit your head. Don't you remember?"

She licked her lips. "When I left to go on my *rumspringa,* you never came to find me when I stayed in New York. It's okay. I'm not mad, I just want to know why."

He sat down beside her and picked up her hand again and she felt the warmth of his touch. "You never went on *rumspringa.* You changed your mind when I took you to the bus stop. You had this whole notion that you were going to become a famous supermodel, and you could've done it if you'd wanted to, but you changed your mind and never got on the bus."

It all made sense. She knew she would've ended up marrying Derek and having children and living in a sweet little storybook house. Letting go of his hand, she picked up her mug with one hand and pinched herself with the other until it hurt. She still didn't wake up.

"Heidi!" He shook his head. "What are you doing?"

"Trying to wake up."

He leaped to his feet. "That's it. I'm taking you to the doctor."

"No, I'm fine."

"*Nee,* you're not. You're even speaking in a weird way. You're not yourself. I'll book an appointment and hopefully we can get you in to see him today." He strode out of the room.

Heidi continued drinking coffee. If he was insisting on taking her to the doctor, she'd have to make sure she didn't give them any reason to declare her insane. Even if she was having a dream, she didn't fancy it turning into that sort of a nightmare.

Feeling like a fat useless frump, she headed back to look at the small baby. He had wiggled his wrapping loose, and waved his arms around while his lips moved as well. Heidi stared at him in wonder while his tiny fists opened and closed. Reaching down, she touched his soft skin and then one of his hands encircled one of her fingers and he slowly turned his head and looked at her.

"Hello, little baby." The baby opened his mouth as though to answer and started wailing. "It's okay, don't cry." She picked him up and held him close against her shoulder and then patted him on his back. "You must be hungry, too." Holding him with one hand, she pulled a small blanket off the edge of the crib and wrapped it around him, and then left the bedroom. As soon as she was out the door, she saw stairs. Slowly and carefully she made her way down them.

"It sounds like he's hungry," she said to Derek when she found him in the kitchen.

"I've got his bottle warming. It won't be much longer."

"Thank you."

He glanced over at her and it was then she realized she wasn't speaking in Pennsylvania Dutch.

"I've made an appointment at the doctor for twelve."

"For me?" She jiggled the baby up and down, trying to stop his crying.

"*Jah*, for you."

"That was fast." She only hoped that she would wake up before then. She wasn't a fan of doctors. When the baby stopped crying, she took her chance to say some things to Derek. Maybe he was having the same dream about her and would remember it when he woke. "I want to apologize for leaving. I never realized what we had."

"You never left me, Heidi."

"If I had, I would've been silly. That's what I meant and I just wanted you to know that."

He moved closer to her and put one arm around her. She closed her eyes and nuzzled into his manly chest while the baby was nestled between the two of them.

"I never would've let you go," he said.

"Really?"

"*Jah.*"

She took a step backward. "So, let's just say that I'd gone on *rumspringa* when I was eighteen, and then decided to stay away, would you have come to find me?"

"*Nee.*"

She stepped back again. "*Nee?*"

"That's right."

She pouted. "Why not?"

"*Gott* gives everyone a free will to choose what they want in life. If you had chosen to leave, I would've had to respect your decision. Do you understand that?"

Heidi was disappointed with his reasoning.

"What would you have done if I had left?" he asked.

"I would've been angry with you and I'd have wondered why you left me."

"Would you have come after me?" he asked.

Slowly, she shook her head.

He smiled at her. "Why?"

"I would've been too afraid of what I'd find when I got there, if that makes sense. I'd have been afraid you wouldn't want me and I would've gone all that way for nothing." Now she had a better idea why he hadn't chased after her. "I would've just hoped that you would've come back of your own accord because you would've missed me so much."

He chuckled. "I could never have done that. I could never have left you." He stared at her for a moment. "And?"

He was waiting for her to say she could never have left him either. She had regretted it, but staying with him would've meant staying within the community and leading a boring life. Being back in his arms had certainly made her rethink her choices. "I would've been a fool to leave you." And that was the truth.

He chuckled once more and held her close again. Then the baby yelled once more, and shattered the moment. "The bottle's coming, little *bu*. It should be warm now." He left them to get the bottle out of the saucepan.

Heidi giggled at the way he spoke to the baby. "He can't understand you, so there's no use talking to him."

He wiped the bottle off and laughed. "You were the one who told me to talk to our *bopplis* and then they'll start understanding."

"That's true. Do you want to feed him?"

"Okay. Your eggs are there," he nodded to the table while he took the baby.

They both sat down at the kitchen table, keeping warm by the stove. She ate the food he had prepared for her while he fed the baby. She looked around the kitchen and it affirmed to her how real everything seemed including Derek and the baby. Could she have hit her head and dreamed her other life? Was this her real life and the other was just a dream—a fantasy? "I need to make a phone call." She had memorized Janelle's number just in case she ever lost her own phone.

"Who do you need to call?"

"Just a friend."

"Do you have to do that now? You haven't even finished eating."

"Oh." She looked down at the eggs on the plain white china plate. *"Denke."* She spooned some more into her mouth.

"Don't go making any plans with your friends. Remember we've got the doctor at twelve."

"I won't forget." To be polite, she finished her eggs and then headed outside, hoping there would be a phone in the barn. When she was outside, she saw a shanty that housed a phone. Her hands were cold and shaky as she dialed her friend's number. When she heard the phone had connected and she was getting a dial tone, her heart pumped hard. It was a real phone number and that meant she wasn't dreaming.

"Hello, this is Janelle Adams."

"Janelle, it's me."

"Who is it?"

"It's Heidi."

"Hello, Heidi. How are you?"

Heidi could tell by how she spoke that Janelle didn't recognize her name or her voice. Janelle didn't know who she was at all. She tried something else. "Are you in the office?"

"I'm out of the office at the moment. How can I help you?"

"Do you know who this is?" There was hesitation on the other end of the line. "Janelle, who do you work for?"

"Our Town Blinds and Awnings."

Janelle wasn't even a realtor and she was going by her maiden name, when she'd almost immediately changed all her business cards and everything else to her married name. "Is this some kind of a joke?" Heidi asked.

"Can I help you with something? Do you need a quote on blinds?"

"Janelle, do you know me—Heidi King?"

"I'm sorry the name doesn't ring a bell, but I meet hundreds of people every week. I'm sorry. Do you need—"

She tried something else since her married name would've been Miller. "Heidi Miller."

"I'm sorry—"

Heidi hung up the phone's receiver. If Janelle didn't know who she was then maybe this was her real life and she'd just dreamed her whole entire other New York City life, but if that was so, how did she know of Janelle's existence and, equally mysterious, how did she know her phone number?

If only she could talk to someone. She couldn't talk to Derek because he was taking her to a doctor, and she certainly couldn't talk to the doctor about something like that. She heard a noise and turned to see Derek coming toward her with a heavy black coat.

"You'll catch your death out here, Heidi. Come back inside." He flung the coat over her shoulders, put his arm around her and together they walked back into the house.

"Now sit down in front of the fire and I'll go make you another coffee. I don't like you getting chilled like that."

She looked down at the baby who was propped in a wooden crib with his bottle nearby. She reached down and picked him up, held him in her arms and fed him the rest of his bottle. "Do you know what's going on, little one? Maybe if you were older, I could talk to you. There's no one else I can confide in. Maybe I am going mad. Shh, don't tell anyone." The baby stared up into her eyes while he sucked hard on the bottle.

She said a quick silent prayer. She'd heard of alternate universes. Maybe she had crossed over into one through some kind of portal. She'd listened to the theories and even though she'd always tried to keep an open mind, she never imagined they were a real thing. If that was what was happening, then one version of her was a realtor living amongst the *Englisch,* and the other was a wife and mother living amongst the Amish. If that was what had happened to her, how would she cross back into her other life?

Once the baby was fed, Heidi headed upstairs with him in one arm. If they were going out, she'd have to change out of her nightdress. *No wonder Derek is worried about me. I can't believe I went outside in just my nightie!*

She placed the baby back in the crib and opened her closet. She took out a purple dress. Back in New York, she never wore colors and it was confounding to see an array of colors in an Amish wardrobe. At home, all her clothes were either black or cream, and with her interest in fashion, everything had a designer label.

She looked around for some warm stockings and

finally found them hanging in a bag in her closet. They were thick and boring, but at least they were black. Then her attention turned to her choice of shoes. Once again, all were black, with a choice of either black lace-up boots or black lace-up flat shoes—a far cry from the stilettos she normally wore. Once she'd hunted up clean underwear and stripped off her nightgown, she looked down at her normally flat stomach and wanted to cry. Where had it gone? In its place was a flabby-looking tummy that not even a million tummy crunches and a year's membership to a gym would fix. Doing her best to ignore the sight, she pulled on underwear, dress and stockings. Lastly, she donned and laced up her boots.

The next chore was to braid and pin her hair so it would fit under her *kapp*. The first model agency she'd gone to in New York City had suggested she cut her hair in a shoulder-length bob. She'd kept it like that until recently when she had it cut short into the spiky pixie style. She laughed quietly, wondering what Derek would say to that idea.

It had been years since she had pulled a brush through hair that was way past her thighs. Not only was brushing it a time-consuming chore, once it was tangle-free, she had the job of braiding it. She found bands wrapped around her hairbrush handle, and once she'd woven her hair into two long braids, one at either side of her head, she wound them carefully around her head and pinned them in place. Then she situated her white prayer *kapp* over the top. *Wow. I forgot about doing that every day. I was much quicker at it before I left for New York.*

A strange smell coming from the crib reminded her

SAMANTHA PRICE

that babies needed diaper changes. She'd changed many diapers when she'd looked after babies for their mothers at meetings before she'd left the community, so at least she knew what to do.

She picked up the baby, spied some cloth diapers and went about changing him. "It's a tough job, but someone's got to do it. Your *vadder* has been doing everything for me this morning, so I couldn't ask him to do it."

"See, now you're talking to him too."

She looked over her shoulder to see Derek, and then she laughed. "It just seems normal to talk to him. He and I have an understanding."

"We'll have to enjoy him before he starts talking if he's going to be anything like Molly."

"Yes," she agreed, thinking that Molly must either be cheeky or she must talk a lot. She fastened the clean diaper at the center with one large pin. "There you go, Michael. As good as new."

"Here." Derek stretched out his hand for the diaper. "I'll take it down to the laundry room. And it looks like you're okay without that second cup of coffee."

"*Denke.* And *jah,* I am okay. I got caught up in getting dressed and forgot about it.

She placed the baby back in the crib and went to find the bathroom, which thankfully wasn't too far from the bedroom. When she was a young child, they hadn't had a bathroom in their house. A bathroom had been installed indoors when she was around ten years of age. These were all the things that had never occurred to her in her day-to-day life. Back home, she'd never thought to be grateful to step out of her bedroom into a fully functioning bathroom. She was more worried about how stylish and up-to-date it was, rather than being grateful that she had one indoors.

Once she'd used the toilet and had a quick wash, she worried about the older children. Surely they'd notice she was different and she wouldn't remember things about them. Derek thought she was suffering memory loss, so she had to go along with that. Maybe before she even got to see them, she might be back in her other life. Then it occurred to her that she should make the most of her time with Derek and also enjoy what came with being a mother.

HEIDI STAYED IN THE BEDROOM, too frightened to speak to Derek in case he thought she was losing her mind.

Several minutes later, Derek poked his head through the door, giving her quite a fright. "I'm going to do some work in the barn, and I'll call out just before we need to leave. Is that all right?"

"Yes, that's fine." She cleared her throat. *"Jah,* that's fine," she corrected herself; it'd taken her a long time to forget about using Pennsylvania Dutch, and now she had to remember to use it. *Jah* hadn't seemed so odd, as many Americans used ya instead of yes, but the other words and phrases had drawn some pretty interesting looks until she worked them out of her speech patterns.

He smiled at her, and then said, "Can I get you anything?"

"Nee, denke. I'm fine." She'd forgotten how handsome he

had been as a young man, and he looked even better and more masculine now that he was older. It seemed unfair that men looked better once they got older. Her looks had gone downhill, and she had avoided the small cosmetic investments her peers back in her real life made to keep their youthful looks.

Derek gave her a little nod and left the room. She listened to his footsteps as he made his way down each wooden step. When she heard him close the front door, she looked out the window and watched him walk to the barn. Now she was free to have a look around the place. There was something about the house that was oddly familiar and she was certain she'd been there before.

The first room she explored was the living room. It was the rough stone fireplace that looked familiar. The rough-cut stones were large and of a sandy-color, stacked one upon the other. The fireplace was topped with a large piece of dark wood forming the mantel. There was a pretty white china clock centered on it.

She sank down onto the couch, liking the way it molded to her body. Soft, but not too soft. There was a three-seater couch opposite, and one comfortable-looking arm chair beside it, with a low table in between all of them. Covering the bare floorboards was a large braided rug in muted grays and reds.

Over the back of the couch was a crocheted throw, and a pile of children's toys were stacked in the corner. A faint smell of smoke from the fireplace completed the homeyness of it all. A smiled twitched at her lips. It was a perfect room for a family to sit around the fire on cold winter's nights, drinking hot chocolate and telling stories.

Maybe her life would've been happy if she stayed within the Amish community and married Derek. She could get used to this life if she had to, but could she really live without the modern-day basic necessities? The computer kept her connected and television was the way she wound down every night. She pressed her back into the couch and looked up at the ceiling.

Reminding herself she'd have to do a good job of fitting into this lifestyle while she remained there, she headed back into the kitchen. There she opened every drawer, every cupboard and every cabinet, and looked through the gas-powered refrigerator. As an Amish woman, she was in charge of the food, so it was good to see what they had because she'd soon be expected to cook.

She could see there were no bedrooms downstairs, so she climbed the stairs to have a look in all the bedrooms. The first bedroom at the top of the stairs contained a single bed. The room was spotlessly clean, with a sizeable blue and gray rug on the floorboards and partway under the bed. Trying to guess the age of the girl who occupied the room, she opened the closet door. She ran her hands along the hanging dresses. There were two in different shades of green and one in deep blue. Going by the size of the clothing, she figured the girl would be around seven years of age.

She closed the closet and moved to the next room. Another single bed. The clothes in that room were a little smaller. "The younger sister. There's only two of them." There had to be only two because there were no more bedrooms upstairs. After she closed that closet door, she looked around the room. It was pretty much the same setup as the other one, with the bed under the window, and a medium-sized brown and green rug on the bare floorboards. The only difference was that this room had more toys and they were stacked on a low bookcase. She crouched down to look at the toys and saw they were all intricately carved. Derek had loved woodwork, she remembered as she pushed herself to her feet. Had he made these beautiful things for his daughter?

The only other bedroom was the large bedroom she shared with the baby and Derek.

There was only the one bathroom, but she wasn't about to complain. At least there was one within the house. She made her way downstairs feeling like she was on an episode of Wife Swap—she was completely out of her depth, and she didn't even have a manual to see how the household ran. She'd have to make it up as she went along.

Exploring downstairs, she found the laundry room just off from the mudroom, which led off from the large kitchen. The house was adequate; no luxury items anywhere, but it suited the needs of a small Amish family.

CHAPTER 4

"Are you ready, Heidi?"

"I'm coming." She walked over to the baby who was still sleeping, wrapped him in an extra blanket and picked him up. He opened his eyes and looked at her and then cried. "It's okay, baby. We can have a ride in the buggy. Isn't that exciting?" He stopped crying and stared into her eyes. It gave her an uncanny feeling as a sudden rush of love overcame her. She told herself not to get attached, but she feared it was too late for that. Eventually, she'd have to leave him when she woke up, or crossed back into her other reality.

She walked downstairs with Michael in her arms and saw Derek waiting for her in his black hat and thick black coat.

"Here, give him to me while you put your coat on."

She liked the way he was so protective and caring. She handed the baby over, and while she was putting on her coat, she said, "What about a bottle for him?"

"You haven't prepared one?"

"*Nee.*" She felt like a failure.

"We've got time."

"*Denke.*" She hurried back into the kitchen remembering they'd also need to take diapers along. When she came back with a bottle, Derek gave her a curious look as she took the baby back into her arms.

"Ready?"

"*Jah.* Except for the diapers. I left them upstairs."

"We'll just use the diapers we keep in the buggy."

"Good idea."

He smiled at her and opened the front door. She stepped out on to the porch and he closed the door behind them. The buggy and a large black horse were waiting for them. When she climbed in, she saw it was fitted out with a heater. That was a luxury. Back when she'd left the communities very few buggies had heaters in them. She got comfortable and fed Michael his bottle.

Once they left the driveway, she looked back at the house and she knew why it was so familiar. They were living in old Mrs. Henderson's house, and it'd been extensively renovated since last time she was there. She gazed back at the road over the top of the handsome shiny black horse. His head was held high and his long mane and tail swished majestically in the cold wind as he clip-clopped along at a steady pace.

She leaned back into the leather seat and closed her eyes. It was a slow mode of transport, but she found herself relaxing. She would've allowed herself to relax even more if she hadn't been going to the doctors. This doctor probably knew her, and she would have to pretend she knew him as well and she just hoped she could pull it off.

"You're very quiet," Derek said as he looked over at her.

"I'm just relaxing. It's cozy here in the buggy."

"You're warm enough? There's a blanket in the back."

"I'm nice and warm thanks to the heater."

He chuckled. "That's good."

Many people didn't like the bitter cold winter, but Heidi loved it. She loved being huddled warm and cozy beside a fire. She didn't have a fireplace in her apartment as it had central heating. Nothing was as good as an open fire.

When they came into the small town, he pulled into the parking lot of the doctor's office. She had been there before, but the doctor she'd been to would have long since retired. She was pleased, at least, that she wasn't going to the hospital to see a doctor. It was much less intimidating to go to a small doctor's practice.

They walked into the waiting room and as Heidi sat down with Michael, Derek told the receptionist they were there. He turned around, smiled at her, and sat down with them. His warm and easy manner always made her feel safe. "You'll be going in soon, he said. "I'll take Michael."

Carefully she passed their baby over. She was getting used to the feel of him in her arms, but still, she didn't want to get attached. She sat there staring at the fish tank watching the goldfish making their way through the water. It reminded her about the conversation she'd recently had with Janelle about owning a pet.

That got her to thinking; when she got back to her other life would she remember she'd been in this one?

Would it be like a dream that she remembered? Now that she had been in this life, would she be able to cross from one to the other? She didn't know if she could do that. She just wanted to get back to her old life where she felt like she belonged. But right now, whatever was going on, she had to do the best job she could of fitting in.

The doctor stepped out of his office. "Mrs. Miller."

She looked up to see a doctor in his fifties with wiry gray hair and thick black eyebrows. She glanced back at Derek and he gave her a reassuring smile.

"You'll be okay. I'm just out here."

She nodded and then headed into the doctor's office.

"How have you been?" he asked when both she and he had sat down.

"I've been a bit tired and my mind's been a bit foggy."

He nodded. "That tends to happen after a baby and even during pregnancy."

"Other than that, I'm fine."

"I'll start with checking your blood pressure." While he was taking her blood pressure, she said, "It was my husband who thought I should come to see you. I feel fine. There's nothing to worry about."

The doctor shushed her and both remained silent until he took the strap off her arm. "There. Now it's okay to talk. Your blood pressure's fine."

"That's good. I was sure it would be."

"Did everything go okay with the birth?" he asked.

This must've been the first time she'd visited him after the baby was born. "Everything went fine."

"No concerns?"

She shook her head. "None."

"When your husband made the appointment this morning, he mentioned you hit your head and suffered some memory loss."

She swallowed hard. "I was just a bit vague, that's all. I didn't lose my memory." She wondered if she was doing the right thing keeping information from him, but she was too scared to tell him the truth.

"How did you come to hit your head?"

"I fell and hit my head on one of the steps on the front porch. The stairs were wet and slippery and I was rushing to get the girls out of the rain." She shrugged her shoulders. That was all she'd been told. "That's all."

"Let me feel the bump where you hit your head."

"Okay, I guess." The doctor had her remove her *kapp*, and gently ran his fingers over the back of her head. She flinched "Ouch. That's a little tender."

"I'm not surprised. It feels like quite a bruise, but the bone seems intact. Were you unconscious at any time? Did you black out?"

That was a question she couldn't answer. She gave the safest answer. "No. I slept a lot afterward though, according to my husband."

He stared at her, looking confused.

"I mean, I wasn't keeping an eye on the time, so I didn't know how long I slept."

He nodded, and then wrote something down. "I'm sending you to the hospital for tests. You could have a mild concussion."

"No, I won't go to the hospital."

He stopped writing and looked up at her. "You won't?"

"Absolutely not."

AMANTHA PRICE

"Does that have something to do with your faith?"

She nodded.

"I know some Amish people happily go to the hospital, but if you don't want to, I can't force you."

She nodded, relieved, and she just wouldn't mention to Derek that he had wanted her to go to the hospital.

"If you start vomiting or feeling dizzy, you'll need to call an ambulance. Okay?"

"I will."

He dipped his head and stared at her from underneath his bushy black eyebrows. Heidi almost giggled because he was giving her a "*Mamm* look."

"I mean it, Doctor, I will," she said. "I need to be healthy for my family."

"That's right. You need to take it easy over the next few weeks."

"I will, and the memory had nothing to do with the bump on the head. I have been a little vague. It's just that I have so much to think about, and with the new baby I've been very tired. I've hardly been getting any sleep."

"That's a common problem with new mothers. The best I can suggest is that you need to sleep when the baby's sleeping."

She guessed what a new mother would say. "It's hard, because that's the only time I can get anything done."

"Relax your housekeeping standards until you catch up on your sleep."

She nodded. "I will."

"Well, that's all for today. Unless there's anything else I can help you with?"

0

She sprang to her feet. "No, thank you. That's everything."

"Please remember what I said."

"I will."

She headed out to Derek feeling relieved, and was happy to tell Derek she was fine. He passed her the baby while he paid for the appointment.

On their way out of the office, he asked, "Are you sure you're fine?"

"*Jah*. I'm overtired and he said it was normal to be vague. He said I might have a mild concussion and if I feel sick I must call the paramedics. He took my blood pressure and it's fine."

"Good. Do you mind if we call in on Ben's store?"

"That's okay." She wondered if he was talking about Ben, his older brother, or a different Ben.

"I've got a few boxes of toys in the buggy for him. You do remember that I agreed to work with him for a few days leading up to Christmas?"

"That's right." She smiled at him

"Only if you're feeling better."

"I told you, I'm fine."

"Good." A few blocks down the road he pulled up. "You might as well come in. I might be here for a while." He helped her step down with the baby, and then said, "You go on ahead."

She looked around not knowing where the store was and then she saw a sign pointing down a side road. Looking closer she saw it read, "Amish Arts and Crafts." Since it was the only sign for an Amish store, she figured that had to be it. She started walking that direction.

Outside the store were small pieces of Amish furniture, and in the window was a rocking horse surrounded by an assortment of wooden toys. They sat on an Amish quilt, and another Amish star quilt was a stunning backdrop for the window display. With one arm, she pushed the door open and was immediately enveloped in warm air.

A woman came out to meet her and Heidi immediately recognized her. It was Faith, an old friend of hers from before she'd left the community.

CHAPTER 5

"HEIDI, Derek told us how you hit your head. Are you all right?" She leaned over and kissed Heidi on the cheek, and then smiled at Michael, who was now fast asleep.

Heidi giggled. "I'm fine. He tends to overreact. I've just been to the doctor and he says I'm okay."

Faith kept staring at Michael. "That's good. And here *he* is. Can I have a hold?"

"Sure." Heidi passed the baby over.

Faith cradled the baby in her arms and swayed her body to and fro, looking like she'd done that many times before. "You've just been to the doctors, just now?"

"*Jah.* We've just come from there now. Derek's bringing toys in."

"Ah, good. I'll just let Ben know he's coming in. How many boxes has he got?"

"He just said a few. I'm not sure how many that means." Heidi guessed her friend had married Derek's older brother.

Faith fetched Ben from the back room and on his way

out, he nodded hello to Heidi. Then Derek appeared at the doorway carrying two boxes, one on top of the other. Derek passed the boxes to Ben and went back to the buggy for more.

"Where are the girls?" Faith asked Heidi.

"They're at *Mamm's* today. We're fetching them later."

Derek came in with another box in time to overhear the conversation. "We're heading off to get them soon and then staying for dinner."

A cold shiver ran through Heidi. She was about to come face-to-face with the parents who'd cruelly cut her off as though she'd never existed. How could she face them? In this life, though, they hadn't disowned her because she'd done everything expected of her. She had married her childhood sweetheart, she kept a nice home, had babies and supported her husband in his work. In her opinion, the real test of a parent's love was always being there no matter what. She was nervous about what she'd find when she saw them.

"How many more boxes have you got, Derek?" Ben asked him.

"Two more."

When customers came through the door, Faith passed the baby back to Heidi. Heidi wandered around at the back of the store looking at all the items. Christmas always used to be such a happy time and all the items she saw reminded her of the gifts she'd received as a child.

When the customers were gone, Faith said, "Heidi, how about you come for dinner tomorrow night?"

"That would be lovely, but I'll have to check with Derek first."

Derek walked into the room, again overhearing what Heidi said. "Check with me about what?"

"Dinner tomorrow night," Faith said. "At our *haus.*"

"That's fine with me."

Heidi smiled at Faith. "We'd love to come."

"Good. We'll look forward to it."

Just then a group of people filled the store. They looked like they were from a tour bus.

"Okay, are you ready?" Derek asked her.

She swung around to look at her husband. *"Jah."*

They waved goodbye to Ben and Faith who were both busily preparing to serve all the customers.

"They look like they're going to be run off their feet," Heidi said.

"They get busier than that. That's why they're going to need me here."

"I'm okay; you should help them now if you want."

"I will, but not today. I just want to make sure you're okay first. If you still don't want to be left on your own tomorrow, they'll find someone else."

Don't want to be left on my own? Was she having some kind of a breakdown? She shook her head. "I keep telling you I'm fine."

They headed back to the buggy, and as they drove away, Derek said, "Do we need any food now that we're so close to the markets?"

"I don't think so. We've got enough food for the time being." She felt smugly pleased with herself for checking the food situation earlier in the day. They didn't have much meat, but perhaps the family preferred not to eat much. Then it dawned on her that they may not be able to afford much meat, and they might be on a strict budget.

"Should we take something to your *mudder's* for tonight?"

She swallowed hard. She wasn't ready to see her parents again. "I suppose we could get a cake, or something."

"Cakes are always a good idea. And then we can get you one of your caramel lattes with the three shots of caramel for the drive home."

She giggled at the kind of coffee she liked. It sounded awful. "That sounds good." She liked caramel, but not in her coffee. Maybe she needed the energy from all that sugar in this life. It occurred to her that if this life was real, that meant she was able to cross between alternate universes, so why had she never done it before? Or, was there some other explanation?

Derek looked down at Michael in her arms. "Sleeping again? What a *gut* life he has."

Heidi giggled. "Eating, sleeping, and being carried around. It is indeed a *gut* life."

"You're sounding a lot brighter."

"*Jah,* I'm feeling good." As they both looked at the road ahead, she worried about her older children. How easy would they be to look after? She reminded herself that most Amish children were well-behaved. They were always raised strictly.

When they walked into the markets, Heidi saw little had changed in the time she'd been gone. Even many of the stallholders were the same, except older. She stayed back a little, and followed Derek until he stopped at a cake stall. Heidi's mouth watered as she looked over the varied assortment of frosted cakes and pies.

"I'll let you choose." Derek said, seeming to be just as lost in the array of cakes as she was.

"There's too much choice."

"Hmm. It'll have to be between the chocolate mud cake and the peach pie."

Heidi said, "What about apple? I say we should go with the apple pie because that's *Dat's* favorite."

"Don't you think that'll make your *mudder* sad?"

"Why would it make her sad?"

She looked into Derek's face and gasped. She realized that her father was no longer with them. It had never entered her head that one of them might have died. She could feel the tears welling behind her eyes.

Before the tears spilled down her cheeks, she handed Michael over to Derek. Then she remembered; the restrooms were on the other side of the markets. Without a further word, she hurried to find them. She walked on and on, trying to keep the tears contained. Finally, she reached her destination and pushed the door open.

As soon as she closed the stall door behind her, the tears ran down her face. She grabbed a handful of tissue to blot the tears. It'd been years since she'd seen her parents. and to learn that one of them had died seemed impossible. It didn't seem real. This life was getting weirder by the minute and too far removed from her normal life to feel comfortable.

So many questions ran through her mind. Is that why her parents hadn't contacted her? Because her father had died and *Mamm* didn't know how to tell her? And why hadn't anyone else told her? She didn't even get the chance to go to his funeral.

After crying for a solid five minutes, she blew her nose, unlocked the door of the toilet cubicle, and looked in the mirror above the washbasin. Her face was flushed red and her eyes were swollen. It was obvious she'd been crying. After she washed her hands and splashed cold water on her face, she knew she'd have to leave the restroom and face Derek. He'd want to know why she didn't know about her father.

She pushed the door open and was faced with Derek, holding the baby and a box.

She smiled at him.

"Better?" he asked.

She pressed her lips together and nodded.

He had the baby securely in one hand and with the other, he held up the white box by its string. "I got the chocolate cake."

She swallowed and nodded. "Good choice."

"Come on, let's go home."

She kept her head down as they walked out of the farmers market. On the way home Derek asked the question she'd been waiting for. "Why didn't you remember your *vadder* had died?"

With her head hung low, she said, "I can't answer that."

"But the doctor said you were okay, *jah?*"

"That's right."

He shook his head. "I don't know how that could be." He glanced over at her. "Did you tell him everything?"

"*Jah.*"

"I should've come in with you."

"He mentioned I might have a slight concussion. That's why he said if I feel nausea or get excessively sleepy, I should call the paramedics. I haven't felt like that at all apart from the general sleepiness, and that's only because of the lack of sleep I've been getting lately." She glanced at Derek hoping she hadn't been speaking too quickly.

"But he's been sleeping through the night for a couple of weeks now."

"I'm still catching up," she said. "Are we going to *Mamm's* now?"

"I thought we'd go there at around five."

"Good idea." She would have a few hours to herself to figure out what was going on before she met her mother again. It wouldn't be the same without her father there.

"Oh, we didn't get your coffee."

"Don't worry about that. That's the last thing—"

"*Nee,* I know how much you enjoy them. We'll stop at the little café you like on the way home."

"*Denke.*" She glanced at him. No one had gone to that much trouble for her over anything. It was nice to have a man to look after her. Derek was just as attentive now as he'd been when they were courting so many years ago. If only she'd realized what she was walking away from. It was comforting to know that he hadn't changed after marriage.

He parked the buggy and then hurried in to get her take-out coffee while she and Michael remained in the warmth of the buggy. She could get used to this life. It was nice to be free of the constant worry and pressures of the real estate business. There was always some drama unfolding or some pitfall to be avoided.

He climbed back into the buggy and put the drink in a little holder next to the heater.

"A cup holder!"

He glanced over at her. *"Jah."*

"That's such a convenience."

He remained quiet and took hold of the reins.

CHAPTER 6

WHEN THEY ARRIVED HOME, she walked into the house realizing that Derek hadn't even locked the door. It was such a different place to live than where she was from. Michael was fast asleep again and Heidi managed to lay him down in the crib in the living room without waking him. Derek had come into the house behind her carrying her coffee.

She took it from him. *"Denke."* After she had a sip, she had to pretend she enjoyed it. It was lukewarm and way too sweet, and the caramel drowned out the coffee flavor. "Delicious," she said.

"Will you be okay if I do some work in the barn?"

"Sure." After Derek walked outside, she sat on the couch with the coffee in one hand and holding her aching head in the other. It wasn't the bump, it was hurting because she was thinking so much about what was happening to her. There was the possibility that she'd gone mad and created that whole other life she had in New York City.

SAMANTHA PRICE

Derek walked back into the house. "I'll fix this fire first." It had just about gone out. "And you left this in the buggy." He handed her the baby's bottle.

She giggled. "I don't know what I'm doing at the moment. *Denke.*"

Derek rearranged the logs on the fire, and added another. He stood up and dusted his hands. "That should do it for a while."

"It looks good."

"I won't be far if you need me."

"I know."

He leaned over and kissed her on her forehead and then headed out the door.

Heidi gazed into the fire and then looked down at her black lace-up boots. She'd dreamed a life quite opposite to the one she had—a life where she wore stilettos and perfectly-fitted designer clothing. She raised her hand to her *kapp.* Even the short spiky haircut she had in her other life was the polar opposite of the long hair she had now.

If this was her real life, wouldn't she'd have some memory of her father's death? It would be hard going to her old home and not having *Dat* there. She sat still, pondering her situation until she heard Michael stirring. Once he was fully awake, she changed his diaper and noticed the clean diaper bundle was low. She made a mental note to do washing tomorrow if she was still there. She'd seen a gas-powered washing machine in the mud room. Thankfully, she wouldn't have to scrub and wash the diapers by hand, but disposables would've been even better.

After she prepared a bottle to take along for Michael, she spent a little time doing some more poking around and looking in cupboards in the kitchen. Then she heard Derek walk into the house.

He poked his head around the kitchen door. "We should leave now. If you're not feeling up to it, I can get the girls and we'll bring you back a cooked meal."

"I'm feeling fine, truly."

"Good. Your *mudder's* expecting us to stay for the evening meal."

Heidi nodded, turning to get Michael and her things. "Did you get some more toys made?"

"I just did some finishing touches and loaded some more boxes ready to take in tomorrow."

"I'm ready to go."

"Let's go then," he said.

They got back into the buggy and traveled to her mother's house, which wasn't that far.

When she walked into the house with Michael in her arms, two young girls ran at her calling out, "*Mamm!*" They were the cutest little girls she had ever seen. They were wearing matching lilac-colored dresses, white aprons and stiff white prayer *kapps*. They reached up trying to hug her and the smaller girl grabbed her around one leg and held on tight.

With Michael in Heidi's arms, she could only give them one-armed hugs.

"Where is *Mammi?*" she asked them.

"She's in the kitchen. Come on." The girls headed back to the kitchen and Heidi followed.

Her mother was there smiling at her and she walked over to her mother and gave her a hug. *Mamm* was so in love with *Dat*, and to lose her husband would've devastated her. Even though she was cranky with her mother, she still held her tightly. *Mamm* had aged, but not too badly. Her face was a little more lined, her complexion a little sallow, and there was considerably more white in her hair.

"Are you better now?" *Mamm* asked. "Is there anything wrong? You haven't hugged me like that for years."

"I've just missed you, that's all."

Derek walked into the kitchen and the girls ran to him. After he said hello to them and took a moment for hugs, he said to his mother-in-law, "Heidi's been to the doctor and he said she's okay." He took Michael from Heidi.

"Good." Her mother looked back at her and eyed her suspiciously, and then spoke to the girls. "Molly and Jessica, both of you, go and set the table."

Derek stood in the doorway of the kitchen while *Mamm* looked Heidi up and down. "You look tired. Go sit in the living room before you fall down. You don't look well to me." She looked up at Derek. "Are you sure the doctor said she's all right?"

"I'm fine, *Mamm*, and you can talk to me. You don't have to talk to Derek about me when I'm here in front of you."

"The doctor said she might have a slight concussion," Derek said.

"It's not life-threatening or anything like that. Please, don't make a fuss."

"Off to the living room with you," her mother said.

Remembering it was no use arguing with her mother, she turned and walked out of the room, and Derek, with the baby, followed close behind. They sat together on the couch by the roaring fire.

Heidi stared into the flames remembering how she used to sit there beside her father years ago. It wasn't the same being in the house with him gone. Besides that, it felt like the foundations of her life had been weakened and that filled her with unrest and uneasiness. She didn't even know how he'd died. Did he have a lingering illness, or was his death sudden, or by accident? She couldn't even ask questions. Then she could no longer hold back the tears.

"Heidi, what's wrong?"

"I'm sad about my *vadder.*" She spoke quietly and wiped her eyes, so her mother wouldn't see her upset.

"We all miss him," Derek whispered

She glanced at him wondering if he'd grow impatient with her. When she saw his kind loving eyes, she knew she didn't deserve him. "Why do you put up with me?"

He smiled. "That's what I'm here for. We help each other. When one's down we lift the other up. It might be me down next week." She wiped her eyes and then her older daughter saw her and came running over. "Why are you crying, *Mamm?*"

"Don't say anything. I don't want *Mammi* to know I'm crying."

"Why?"

"Because I'm sad about your *grossdaddi* dying and if she sees I'm upset, she'll get upset."

The girl pulled out a small handkerchief from her

sleeve. "You always tell me to carry a clean handkerchief and the first time I use it, is to give to you."

"Denke." Heidi smiled at the cute girl as she wiped away her tears.

Seeing her sister with her mother, the younger one ran over and the older one pulled her aside and whispered something to her. The younger one then looked at her mother through big round eyes and walked over. "Remember you told us he's with *Gott?* He's not sad, he's happy. And he's looking down on us with Jesus and they're both smiling."

It warmed Heidi's heart to see how sweet both of the girls were. If that's how good motherhood was, she'd burst with happiness. "That's true. I must stop crying I don't want *Mammi* to see me so upset."

"We won't tell her you've been crying."

"Good girl, Molly," Derek said.

"Denke," Heidi said.

The younger girl, Jessica, Heidi now knew, stepped forward and put her fingers on the sides of her mother's lips and pushed them up into a smile. "We didn't even know him and we miss him too even though we were small when he died."

"I don't even remember him," Molly said.

From the kitchen, Heidi's mother called out, "Have you two finished setting the table?"

"Jah, Mammi," they chorused before they moved back into the kitchen.

Heidi held onto Molly's handkerchief and dabbed at her eyes.

Throughout the meal, Derek held the sleeping baby and managed to eat the meal one handed.

"I've hardly ever seen him awake," Heidi's mother said.

Derek looked down at him. "He's due to wake up soon."

"Is he sleeping through the night yet, Heidi?"

Heidi didn't know the answer to that, but she recalled that Derek said he had been. "Sometimes." She was relieved when Derek went on to explain that in the last week he had slept through the night at least four times.

"Are we going to make cookies again this Christmas, *Mamm*?"

"Molly, what have I told you about talking at the table? Children are to be seen and not heard at the dinner table. You can speak if you are spoken to."

Heidi smiled, remembering *Mamm's* strict rules.

"That's something we can talk about another time, Molly," she said to soften her mother's harsh response.

She was glad she was sitting directly beside *Mamm* because she didn't want her mother to see her eyes and know she'd been crying. The way everyone was acting around her, she was sure they thought she had the baby blues. It was hard to be thrust into motherhood at the deep end. If she stayed in this life, how was she going to be an instant mother to these two older children and the young baby?

After dinner, Heidi tried to help her mother clean up and wash the dishes, but she wouldn't hear of it. "Young *mudders* need their sleep. I don't have anything better to do. The washing up isn't keeping me from anything."

"*Denke, Mamm.* Are you sure?"

SAMANTHA PRICE

"Jah, go home and get a good night's sleep."

Heidi leaned in and hugged her mother. *"Denke* for looking after the girls today."

"You must learn to look after yourself. You have to be well to look after your family."

Heidi nodded. "I know."

ONCE THEY WERE BACK HOME, it was bedtime for the girls.

"Mamm, we're not tired and there's no school tomorrow."

"Molly, you must stop arguing."

"Mamm's right. You still have to go to bed, school or no school."

"Can we have one horsey ride, *Dat?"*

Heidi looked over at Derek and smiled.

"Sit on the couch and watch, *Mamm,"* Jessica said.

It was then that Heidi realized what the game was about. She sat on the couch, and then Derek said, "One ride each and then it's off to bed for both of you. No coming down for a drink of water and no coming back down to say good night three times, okay?"

When both girls nodded, Derek got down on all fours and whinnied like a horse. The girls were delighted and broke out into shrieks of giggles. Then he pounded his pretend hoof on the floor and snorted.

"You go first, Jessica," Molly said pushing her sister forward.

"I'm scared of the wild horse," said Jessica. "What if he bites?"

68

Derek showed his teeth and continued to pound the ground.

Molly pushed Jessica forward again, and she jumped onto her father's back. Once she was on properly, he galloped back and forth in front of the fire and then he reared up and she slid off.

Heidi loved the way Derek was playing with the girls and being silly. Then Molly ran and jumped on his back when he was still on all fours. He reared up and Molly managed to hang on.

Molly patted him on his neck. "It's okay, horsey. I'm not gonna hurt you."

Derek sidestepped and whinnied again while Jessica shrieked with delight.

"Hang on, Molly," Jessica said.

Then Derek took her once around the living room and stopped back in front of Heidi.

"More, more," Molly said giggling.

"That's it for tonight," Derek said.

"*Nee,* more," Molly said.

"That's it," he said firmly.

Molly slid off. "Nice, horse. Here's a carrot for being so good."

Jessica stepped up and held out her hand too. "And I've got a lump of sugar for you."

Derek pretended to eat off their hands.

"That's it. Off to bed with you," Heidi said. "The horse needs to go to sleep as well."

Derek stood up and scooped the girls up, one in each arm and carried them up the stairs. Heidi pulled the crocheted blanket off the back of the couch, spread it over herself and hugged it. The bond with her girls was imme-diate and that was something she hadn't expected. She hadn't needed to worry about not fitting in with them. More and more, Derek was proving to be the perfect man and she'd fallen even more in love with him when she saw him with their children.

CHAPTER 7

Tuesday, December 19

HEIDI WOKE up the next morning and looked around. She was still in the Amish home with her new and instant family. Derek appeared in the room, startling her a little. He had on his hat and coat.

"I didn't want to leave without saying goodbye." He walked closer, leaned down and gave her a quick kiss on her forehead.

"I just woke."

He glanced over at the baby. "It's good to see that Michael's sleeping so much at night now."

She sat up and stretched her arms above her head. "*Jah*, it's good to get a full night's sleep for a change."

Derek smiled at her. "I'll see you this afternoon."

"Bye."

He walked out and then Heidi was filled with fear. How would she cope on her own with three young children? She'd looked after young children before, but it was many years ago, back before she'd left the community, and she didn't have the responsibility of being the mother then. Heidi stayed in bed thinking and worrying, until she heard cooing sounds coming from the crib. She walked over to Michael and looked in; she was sure he was smiling at her. "Good morning, young Michael." She lifted him up and kissed him on the top of his nearly bald head. "Let's change your diaper and then I'll give you some breakfast. Would you like that?"

When she was sitting down in the living room and feeding him his bottle, she heard footsteps hurrying down the stairs. Both girls ran to her and then started kissing Michael and trying to hug him. With their *kapps* off, their light brown hair fell down to their waists. Their long-sleeved nightdresses made them look very old-fashioned.

"I'll make you breakfast in a minute. As soon as Michael finishes his bottle. Sit by the fire to keep warm."

"Can I give him his bottle if I sit up straight?" Molly asked.

"Not right now. Maybe later."

"Why not now?" she asked.

"*Nee.* Because I say so."

"Has *Dat* gone to work already?" Molly asked next.

"*Jah.*"

"What does he have to work for?" Jessica asked.

"He has to help your *onkel* in his store for Christmas because they're very busy with everyone buying Christmas presents."

"What are we getting *Dat* this year?" asked Molly.

She bit her lip. She hadn't even thought about

presents. Back home she only gave out bonuses at Christmas time. "What would you girls like to give him?"

Molly shrugged her shoulders. "I don't know."

"Let's go shopping and find something special," Jessica said.

"Maybe." Heidi said, figuring she'd have to do something.

"*Dat's* got the buggy, *Mamm*," Molly reminded her.

"That's true. Maybe we can take it tomorrow if we wake up very early. We can take *Dat* to the store and collect him at the store when he finishes. That way, we can use the buggy."

Molly cheered. "I want to get *Dat* a special present."

"Me too," Jessica said.

Heidi smiled at the two of them. "We should do that tomorrow, then." Heidi looked at Michael and when she saw he was asleep, she pulled the bottle out of his mouth and placed him in his downstairs crib. "Okay, breakfast time."

The girls followed her to the kitchen where she found eggs along with half a loaf of bread. She made them the favorite breakfast *Mamm* used to make for her when she was a child—bread slices soaked in eggs beaten with a little milk and then fried until they were golden brown. Her mother had called it French toast.

The girls loved it. After breakfast was done, Heidi said to the girls, "Get dressed and then put your coats on. Once you've done that, we'll have a look in the barn."

"What for?" Jessica asked.

"Just because I want to have a look, that's why. Must you always ask questions?"

"I'm only little, and that's how I learn things."

"Let's go, Jessica," Molly pulled her sister by the sleeve. "I'll help you with your hair."

They were downstairs a few minutes later. *"Gut.* Now, Molly, put your coat on and then help your *schweschder* put hers on."

"I can do it by myself," Jessica said.

WHILE HEIDI PULLED on her coat, she watched the young girls put theirs on. "See what you can do when you try?"

"I've always been able to dress myself," Jessica said. "I'm not a *boppli."*

Jessica's words told Heidi she was treating her as though she were younger.

"Do we need to do them up?" Molly asked.

"Nee. That should be fine. We're just going to have a quick look around the barn."

"What are we looking for?" Molly asked.

"Nothing in particular. I just want to see what's there in case it needs cleaning or something like that." Heidi had a last look at the baby, who was still fast asleep and then headed out to the barn. "Both of you stay by me. Don't go running off anywhere and don't touch anything."

"We won't, *Mamm."*

"Nee, we won't, *Mamm,"* Jessica echoed.

Heidi pushed the door the barn open and instead of seeing a workshop bench stuck in one corner, the whole left-hand side of the barn was a separate room that had been turned into a workshop. It was separated from the rest of the barn by a wall with two large picture windows and a door. "Your *vadder* went to a lot of trouble to do this." Heidi walked through the doorway with them. "Now neither of you touch anything," she repeated as she stepped backward staring at them.

"We won't, *Mamm*."

When Heidi turned back around, she knocked a tool off the workbench. That sent both girls into squealing giggles.

"You told us not to touch anything, *Mamm*, and then you dropped something."

Heidi leaned over and picked up the metal tool. "I forgot to tell myself." She looked back at the girls as she put the tool back where it had been. "On second thought, both of you just stay there by the door." She left them at the door while she looked at the pieces Derek was working on. She picked up a small wheel that had been fashioned from wood and marveled at the intricate workmanship.

All manner of tools hung neatly on the wall, graded into different sizes. Shelves of toys filled one end of the workshop. She wondered how he'd found the time to make so many. Had he neglected his family to do it? Then she realized that this must've been his full-time job. Maybe that's what he did for a living. She didn't really know.

When she turned to leave, the girls were nowhere to be seen. She turned around to close the door behind her and then she saw Jessica spinning in circles while Molly was playing in the sawdust.

"Let's go," Heidi said. While she walked to the main

barn door, she heard Molly whispering, and she stopped still to try and hear what her daughter said.

"Throw the sawdust around." When Jessica said no, Molly urged her. "Go on. It'll be fun."

Before Heidi even turned around, Jessica was throwing handfuls of sawdust everywhere.

"I heard that, Molly. Stop it, Jessica."

Both girls immediately stood to attention.

"Can't you do what you're told?" She looked from one to the other with a stern face of disapproval.

"We just wanted to play," Jessica said.

"You can play in the house where you won't make a mess."

She then closed the double doors of the barn. Once she had done that, both girls ran to the front door of the house. "Sit by the fire and once you're warmed up, how about we make some cookies?"

The two girls squealed with delight. "Can I help too?" asked Jessica.

"Of course you can. The three of us can make the cookies."

"We're warm now," Jessica said.

The two girls ran ahead of her into the kitchen and when she arrived there, Molly was pulling out a box from the cupboard. She overheard Molly say, "Throw the recipe cards on the floor."

"What are you doing?" Heidi said.

"Getting the cookie recipes."

"No need. I have a recipe in my head."

"How can you have a recipe in your head?" Jessica screwed up her face.

Heidi laughed. "It's memorized in my head." She tapped her forehead.

"You've remembered the whole recipe?" Molly asked.

"That's right. I heard what you said, Molly, and it's not nice to try getting your *schweschder* into trouble."

"I wasn't."

"There is no use denying it. I heard what you said."

"Sorry, *Mamm.*"

"Okay, I forgive you, but don't do it again because you wouldn't like someone to do that to you, would you?"

"*Nee, Mamm.*"

"Good. Now let's forget this happened and move on."

Molly nodded.

"We'll need sugar, butter, milk …" As she said the ingredients, the girls grabbed them and put them on the table. That saved Heidi having to look for them. "Now what about our cookie cutters?"

"Can we use the special star ones?" Jessica asked.

"Of course we can. Those ones are specially for Christmas."

Jessica rummaged around the bottom drawer until Molly pushed her out of the way.

"There it is." Molly plucked out a star cookie cutter and gave it to Jessica and Jessica held it up in the air.

"Here it is," Jessica said, her eyes sparkling.

"Excellent! That was very nice of you to hand it to Jessica, Molly. Will we make all our cookies in star shapes?"

The girls nodded. "They taste better that way," Molly said with a smile from ear-to-ear.

Heidi had no idea how she remembered the recipe

from Agnes's diary, but she recalled it in detail down to the last measurement.

Cookies.

Ingredients.

8 ounces of butter

1 1/4 cups of icing sugar or confectioners' sugar

2 teaspoons of vanilla extract

2 cups of plain flour

1/2 cup of rice flour and

1/3 cup of cornflour (cornstarch)

2 tablespoons full of milk

Method:

Beat butter, sifted icing sugar and extract in large bowl until pale and fluffy. Stir in combined sifted flours into batches then add milk until mixed well.

Divide mixture into half.

Knead each half on a floured surface until smooth.

Shape each half into a ball and keep them loosely covered in a cool place until firm, about an hour.

Preheat oven to medium heat.

Grease the oven trays.

Roll out one ball of dough until ¼ inch thick.

Cut shapes as desired with cookie cutters.

Place on trays one inch apart.

Repeat this process with the second ball of dough.

Collect dough scraps, shape into a ball, roll out and cut out more cookies.

Bake cookies for 8-12 minutes or until golden brown.

Stand on trays for 5 minutes before removing from the oven tray to a tea towel or paper for further cooling. Store in a tightly-sealed container.

HEIDI TAUGHT the girls how to roll out the cookie dough with a floured wooden rolling pin. The two girls then took it in turns, cutting out the stars and placing them on the baking trays while the oven warmed. Heidi sat down on a chair looking around the kitchen while the girls cut the dough. The kitchen was a third of the size of her kitchen back in New York. Here, there were none of the modern conveniences such as dishwasher or food processor.

"All done, *Mamm.*"

Heidi stood. "Ah, there's some left." She pulled the dough leftovers together and they were able to cut out three more star cookies. "Now we put the tray into a moderately heated oven. Not too high or they'll burn, just high enough so they'll bake nicely."

"How long until we can eat some?" Jessica asked.

Heidi giggled. "That's the most important question, but do you think we should leave these for Christmas?" When she saw the girl's sad faces, she changed her mind. "Maybe you can have two each since you worked so hard to make them, and we'll put the rest away until Christmas Day."

Jessica clapped her hands while Molly grinned and nodded.

"That's what we'll do, then." Usually Heidi never

cooked, but if she had, she would've used the timer on her iPhone. It was strange to be back in a kitchen where there wasn't even a stove timer. "See that clock?" She pointed to the small clock next to the stove. "When it's a quarter past, we have to get the cookies out. They'll be done by then."

"Now what?" Jessica asked.

"The washing up, of course. You can wash all that flour and dough off your hands first."

"Do we have to do the washing up?" Molly whined.

"It's all part of cooking."

"It's not cooking though, it's washing up," Jessica said.

Heidi laughed. "It won't take long and washing up can be fun. It's nice to see everything coming up nice and clean."

"I'll wash, it's funner." Jessica said.

"More fun," Heidi corrected her.

Molly said, "You're too little. I have to wash because I'm the biggest."

"You can dry, Jessica, and Molly can wash because her hands can go into hotter water than yours. The hotter the water, the cleaner the dishes will be."

"Okay, I'll dry," Jessica said picking up a tea towel from the countertop.

"Wash your hands first, don't forget." Heidi was pleased that who was washing and who was drying hadn't developed into an argument. She'd had fun baking the cookies with the girls. "While we've got a lot of washing up to do, why don't we make a pie? An apple pie, or a peach cake? Apple was one of your great *grossmammi's* favorites and your *grossdaddi's*."

"Is that in your head too, *Mamm?*"

"*Jah*, it is, Molly. Along with some special little tips on how to make it really good."

"What are tips?"

"Tips are like secrets."

"We're gonna make a secret pie?" Jessica's hazel eyes opened wide. Both girls had the same beautiful eyes as their father.

"*Jah*, let's do it. Leave the washing up for now. We'll make great *grossmammi's* secret peach cake, just the way she used to make it. We don't have apples, but I noticed we do have canned peaches. We'll make that peach cake. Then we'll clean up everything at once."

Peach cake

1 cup flour

1 teaspoon baking powder

2 tablespoons of butter

1 teaspoon of sugar

1/3 of a teaspoon of salt

eight canned or fresh peach halves, reserving juice if using canned peaches

1/4 cup of sugar

1/2 teaspoon of cinnamon

one egg

1/2 cup of milk

reserved peach syrup

Method:

Rub butter into flour, baking powder, salt, and sugar to make fine crumbs.

Press this mixture into a greased round dish, 8 inches in diameter.

Cover with drained peach halves, flat sides down and round sides up.

Sprinkle with combined sugar and cinnamon.

Cook in a moderate oven for 15 minutes.

Take out of the oven

Beat egg and milk until well blended.

Spoon gently over the peach halves.

Return to oven and cook for 30 minutes.

Use the reserved syrup and serve the cake with the syrup as the sauce. To do so, heat the syrup in a saucepan and thicken with 1 tablespoon of cornstarch stirred into 1/4 cup cold water.

CHAPTER 8

THE GIRLS and Heidi had been busy all day in the kitchen, with a couple of breaks to feed, change and play with Michael. Molly and Jessica went upstairs to play together, and Heidi had just sat down when Derek walked in the door.

Heidi made him a cup of hot chocolate and together they sat quietly by the fire.

"It was so busy I didn't get one chance to sit down. I was on my feet all day."

She giggled. "Now you know what it's like to be a *mudder*."

"I already know that. I know it hasn't been easy for you being here by yourself when you've not been well. Was everything okay?"

"It was. We had a fun time making cookies and other things."

"Is that what I can smell?"

Heidi nodded. "And we've got corn on the cob and

vegetable stew for dinner. There wasn't much meat, so I thought we'd save it for—"

"I'm picking up our meat order tomorrow. Don't you remember? You said it'll be enough to see us through Christmas."

"I'm sorry. I forgot," she bit her lip.

"I guess you also forgot we're going to Ben and Faith's place for dinner?"

She tapped her head. "I did. I remembered earlier and then I forgot. Oh well, the stew will be all right for tomorrow night's meal. And maybe I'll brown up the meat and add that to it."

He sipped on his hot drink. "*Jah*, sounds *gut*. Stew is actually better the next day, in my opinion, and I like it best with meat. Now, let's you and I relax a bit. We don't have to leave for another hour."

Instead of relaxing, her nerves kicked in at the idea of seeing Ben and Faith again. What if she was supposed to remember or know things that she didn't? "Okay. I'll get the girls and Michael ready soon. So, what did you sell mainly today?"

"We sold out of most of my toys."

"That's great."

He chuckled. "Christmas is where we make the most money, so I'd be worried if I didn't sell most of them. I've got to take the rest to the store tomorrow. Ben's collecting me just in case you need the buggy tomorrow."

"That's good of you, *denke*. Maybe we will go out somewhere tomorrow. I already told the girls we might. They want to do some shopping." She felt bad because she should've been making things for Christmas rather than shopping. That's what her mother had done with her when she was young. They never got store-bought gifts.

"Only if it's not too cold. Going by the forecast, the weather should be okay tomorrow, but we've got a cold front moving in next week."

Heidi wondered if she'd still be there next week. "Did you enjoy working there? At the store, I mean?"

"It's okay for a change, but I much prefer working here."

She knew he meant in his barn workshop and that confirmed he had made a full-time job out of his wood-working craft. He must make enough for them to live a comfortable life because they didn't seem to lack for anything.

"The girls are very quiet."

"They're playing games in their room. I don't think they heard you come home."

She walked to the stairs and yelled. "Girls, *Dat's* home."

A few seconds later, they were running down the stairs and straight to their father and hugging him.

"And what did you two do today?" he asked.

"We made star cookies," Molly said.

Jessica added, "*Mamm* had a special recipe in her head, and one for pie and one for cake. It's a secret, but it's okay to tell you."

"Is that so?" He turned to look at his wife and she smiled at him. "Do you think I might be allowed to have a cookie before dinner?" he asked Jessica.

"*Jah*," said Jessica, nodding her head while Molly was shaking hers.

"Not before dinner, *Dat,* but you might be able to have one after dinner if *Mamm* says so," Molly said.

"In that case, I'd be happy with one after dinner," he said.

"And the rest are for Christmas day," Jessica told him.

He chuckled, and then Heidi said, "Girls, you can get washed up and change into some good clothes. We're going out to *Onkel* Ben's for dinner."

The girls squealed with delight.

"Tonight?" Molly asked.

"*Jah,* we're leaving in less than an hour. So off you go and get changed."

When the girls headed up the stairs, Heidi asked, "Do you need anything else before we go?"

"*Jah,* please. I need something to keep going. One cookie perhaps?"

She giggled. "Just one."

While she was in the kitchen fetching a cookie, she heard Michael waking from his afternoon nap. She brought Derek two cookies on a small plate and when she entered the room she saw he had Michael in his arms. A warm and happy glow washed over her and she realized she had a husband who loved his wife and children, she had a baby, and a real family. This was how things were meant to be, and now she belonged somewhere, right here, with wonderful people.

He looked over at her. "I think someone's hungry."

"I'll heat his bottle." She placed the plate down on the low table by the couch. When she came back with the bottle, she took Michael from Derek and sat down beside him to feed the baby.

"Why did you forget we were going to Ben and Faith's tonight?"

"You know I'm absent minded sometimes."

"Not usually."

"Sometimes, like today." She giggled to make light of it. "I remembered earlier in the day, and then I forgot once I got busy with the girls and everything. They were quite a handful earlier today."

"Were they?"

"*Jah.* I've noticed that Molly is telling Jessica to do naughty things. I think she's after my attention."

"Who? Molly?"

"*Jah.* I'm probably paying too much attention to Michael, or something."

"They all go through their stages. I wouldn't worry about it too much. Ben always did things like that to me. He thought it was funny to get me into trouble. I got wise to it pretty quickly."

Heidi nodded. Being an only child, she had no idea what siblings did when they were young. "I don't like her taking pleasure in seeing her *schweschder* get into trouble."

"Don't worry too much. Like I said, it's probably just a stage. I did some awful things when I was young and I can't even tell you why."

Heidi hoped that was all it was. Having no siblings herself, she didn't know whether what Molly had done was normal at this age.

BEFORE THEY REACHED Ben and Faith's home, Heidi found out from the excited chatter of her girls in the back seat of the buggy that Ben and Faith had two girls, Sarah and Lily, who were approximately their ages. Carefully set at Heidi's feet was a covered carrying-basket holding the cake they'd made from Agnes's recipe.

When the buggy stopped, Derek cautioned the girls not to run to the house. They were to wait until Heidi got out with the baby, and they would walk quietly and calmly with their mother.

"We won't run, *Dat*," Molly assured him.

"We'll walk slowly," Jessica added.

"Good, see that you do."

When Faith opened the door, Molly stepped forward. "We made a peach cake to bring over."

Heidi reached down and pulled her back slightly, and then said to Faith, "*Jah,* we did. It's in the buggy and—"

"*Dat's* bringing it in." Molly finished her sentence for her as she started unbuttoning her coat.

"That's *wunderbaar.* We love peach cake," Faith said. Then two young girls appeared beside Faith. "Off you all go and play, after you hang up your coats."

"I'm sorry. She's left her manners somewhere today," Heidi said regarding Molly.

Faith swiped a hand through the air. "They're all the same at that age. She'll learn."

Once Heidi was inside, Faith helped her get her coat off, hanging it on a peg by the door. She stared at Michael who was asleep. "Oh, he's so adorable. He's always asleep."

"That's all he does—eats and sleeps. Is there anything I can do? I can give Michael to Derek when he comes in."

"*Nee*, everything is done. I'm just giving the vegetables a few more minutes."

Ben walked into the room, said hello to Heidi and then grabbed his coat, donning it as he went out of the house to see Derek.

"The food smells nice. I don't know how you do it, working full time and then coming home to make a meal."

"Ah, I have a trick for that. I cook a variety of things on my day off and have them in the fridge, and then I can just reheat them as I need them."

"Aha! That's a good idea." That reminded Heidi of how she had her frozen meals prepared ahead of time and all she had to do was pop them in the microwave. The only difference was someone else had cooked them.

"How are you feeling?"

Heidi was a little tired of people asking her how she was. "I'm fine. I really don't think there's anything to worry about. Derek is such a worrier."

"He's just being attentive. Ben is like that, too. We're blessed with good husbands."

"I know. I know, he's so good to me. I'm just tired of all the fussing. "

Just then the two men came inside. They left off talking while Derek handed the cake-carrying basket to Faith as he greeted her, and then he and Ben went into the living room, resuming their outdoor conversation on the way.

The women went into the kitchen, and Heidi pulled out a chair and sat down. Faith set the basket on the counter, peeking inside. "What a beautiful cake. And it smells wonderful, too." She joined Heidi at the table.

"*Denke*. It's my first time to use this recipe. I hope it's good."

"I'm sure it will be. Now, can I have a hold of Michael?"

"Of course you can." She passed him over.

"I'll be so happy when I'm blessed with another *boppli*."

Heidi gave a little giggle. "It'll happen."

"It hasn't happened yet, and you and I had our girls so close together that. when you got pregnant a third time, I thought that I would too. That's how it happened with the others, but I missed out this time."

Heidi nodded. "The right time will come, I'm sure. Have faith," she said with a giggle, bringing a smile to her sister-in-law's face in response to the wordplay. "I didn't have much time to talk to Derek about his day, but I heard you were busy in the store."

"*Jah*, we were. It was one of the busiest days we've ever had and everyone wanted their items gift-wrapped. I was so pleased I had pre-made some boxes last week. That saved us a lot of time today, I can tell you that."

"Good planning on your part. These days, everybody likes saving time. They like to buy gifts and have them wrapped at the same time."

Faith stared at her. "Are you sure you're all right?"

"*Jah*, why?"

"Because you're talking a little differently."

"Oh, I didn't realize. Derek said something along the same lines today."

"I can't quite put my finger on it, but you're saying things you wouldn't normally say."

"I don't know. I just think I'm tired, with the *boppli* and all."

"*Jah*, it's so hard when they're small and you're not getting enough sleep. Are the girls helpful to you?"

"*Jah*, they're a big help. I don't know what I'd do without them."

At that moment, Michael opened his eyes wide and stared up at Faith. The expression on his face made her giggle.

"He likes you," Heidi said.

"Of course he does. He knows I think he's the sweetest baby who ever lived. The sweetest baby *bu,* I should say in case the girls are listening." Faith laughed.

"I don't think they're listening. They're too busy playing with my girls. Are you sure I can't do anything?"

"Nothing needs doing, just relax. I've been meaning to have you here for some time, but there's always been one thing or another standing in the way. With Christmas coming, it would've been well into the new year before we could've gotten together if it wasn't done tonight. Derek has been so helpful at the store. I don't know that we could have managed without him helping today." She looked down at Michael and made faces.

"He does like making his wooden toys with all those moving pieces. It keeps him busy."

Faith looked up at Heidi. "That should be enough time for the vegetables now. I'll find the girls, and I'll take Michael with me if that's okay."

Heidi smiled at the way Faith was taken with Michael. "Of course you can take him."

The dinner was a leg of lamb roasted with several kinds of vegetables. She recalled that the last night in her apartment she'd had a lamb roast meal. Even though Faith admitted that she'd had the meat already cooked, it tasted so much better than the frozen meals Heidi heated in the microwave.

When everything went quiet, Heidi looked around and saw everyone looking at her. It was then she realized someone had just asked her a question. She was certain it was Ben. "I'm so sorry, what was that? I was a million miles away."

Derek said, "Ben was just asking you if you mind if I work at the store on Christmas Eve."

"That's fine, I had expected you would be needed."

"So, you're fully recovered?" Ben asked.

"I feel fine."

"Don't hesitate to call if you're not doing well, and he can come home right away," Ben said.

"I'll keep that in mind, but I'll be fine. There's nothing to worry about."

CHAPTER 9

LATER THAT NIGHT when Derek and Heidi were home and the children were asleep, they sat together on the couch.

"You seemed to have found a new burst of energy tonight," he said as she sat staring at the fire.

"I'm feeling better. I told you I'd get better."

"That's good. And that peach dish of yours was a big hit."

"*Denke,* I was pleased with it, too."

While he read The Budget, one of the Amish newspapers, she sank back into the couch and pulled the crocheted blanket from the back of the couch and spread it over her legs. She thought back to the phone call she'd made to Janelle. If her best friend didn't know her, maybe she was in this life for good. She was worn out from trying to think how she got there and how she would get back. It would've been nice to have just one person in her life in whom she could confide. She gave Derek a sideways glance wondering if she should tell him, and quickly abandoned that idea.

Heidi couldn't confide in her mother, the woman who had cut her off when she'd left the community. If only she'd had siblings, she might've been able to talk with one of them. A huge pop from sap in the log on the fire made Heidi jump, causing Derek to chuckle at the way she reacted.

Then and there she had to accept the fact that maybe she had hit her head and lost her memory, and the life in New York was not real. All those memories and all those people she knew they weren't real. She'd imagined it all when she hit her head, and that bump on the head had wiped out her true memories and replaced them with that other life. She hugged the crocheted blanket close to herself while questioning her sanity. This had to be her real life.

And if this was her real life, she had never climbed on that bus. She'd never become successful and she had never opened her own agency. Could she have imagined her other life because she was deeply unhappy with this one? It seemed unlikely, since she had three beautiful children, and a caring man she was in love with. She glanced sideways at Derek again, so thankful he was the same warm-hearted man he had been as a teenager.

Her life in New York, whether real or imagined, wasn't perfect by any means; she could see that now. Her friends were mostly business acquaintances except for Janelle. At the end of the day she went home to an empty apartment. Smiling, as she looked around, she realized she wanted to call this humble house her home.

"What are you smiling about?" He reached over and pulled her close to him, and she giggled. He kissed her gently just like when they were courting. She pulled back a bit; she wasn't used to being kissed, at least she didn't think she was.

"I'm just thinking about my life."

He folded up his newspaper and put it beside him. "And?"

"We've got a good life."

"I think so."

Just then Molly appeared at the foot of the stairs.

"What have we told you about getting out of bed?" Derek asked sternly.

"I need a drink of water."

"Go back up to bed, and I'll bring one for you."

When Derek got up and went to the kitchen, Molly stared at her.

"Go to bed, Molly." She blew her a kiss. "You heard what *Dat* said."

"*Gut nacht, Mamm.*" Molly smiled, turned and walked slowly up the stairs.

She watched her husband hurry up the stairs with a glass of water for Molly and remembered back to her own childhood when she'd always find one excuse after another to delay bedtime. It wasn't lost on her that Derek had automatically gotten up to get the water for their daughter. Many of her acquaintances were married to men who expected them to do everything with the children and the household, so she was pleased Derek wasn't that kind of man.

Derek sat back down beside her. "What were we saying?"

"I forget."

"I've been meaning to talk to you about Christmas day. Are you still happy to go to my parents' *haus* most of the day?"

Relief washed over her. That would be much less trouble than her having people there for the day. "*Jah*, that's fine."

"And can you make that special dish you always make?"

She slowly nodded figuring, hoping, Molly might help her out with that one by telling her what her special dish was. "Of course. So, we'll have breakfast here, and then go to your parents?"

"That's the plan, after the girls open their presents."

Heidi had no idea what their presents were or even if they had bought them yet. She'd never liked puzzles or guessing games and now she was in the middle of an awkward puzzle. "I must remember to get wrapping paper." She hoped that would prompt him to talk about the gifts and whether they'd been purchased or made yet.

"I thought you and the girls would be making the paper like you usually do."

"Making the paper? I'm not sure …" Now she was in big trouble. She had no idea how to make paper.

"Drawing pictures on the paper." He gave her a quizzical look.

"Ah, yes. I'll have to find out if they want to do that this year. They might be getting a little old for that now." She was relieved when he slowly nodded.

He moved closer, then put his arm around her. Heidi rested her head against his shoulder. It brought back all the feelings she'd had for Derek all those years ago. She closed her eyes and listened to the crackling of the logs burning in front of them. The warm cozy house was a far cry from the cold steel and white marble apartment with its clutter-free clean lines. If she were back home now, she'd be watching the TV. Right at this moment, she much preferred to be cuddling up to Derek and facing the dancing flames in the fireplace.

In her teen years, she'd never intended to stay in the Amish community. Derek had chased her until she agreed to date him and then she had fallen in love with him, but she was sure she'd decided not to let him stand in her way of her dreams. She was certain she got on that bus because she remembered it. She'd waited until everyone had boarded, then she kissed Derek, boarded, and headed to the back seat. When the bus drove off, she definitely remembered she had kept waving to Derek and he'd kept waving to her until the bus turned the corner.

"Do you think Molly was truly thirsty?"

He chuckled. "We forgot to leave her cup of water on the nightstand."

"Ah. We must remember next time."

"At least she's over those dreadful nightmares she used to have," he said.

She bit her lip, not remembering any of it. *"Jah,* they were truly awful."

"You will be all right if I go to work tomorrow, won't you?"

"At the store?"

"*Jah.*"

"We'll be fine. We were okay today making the Christmas cookies and pie."

"If you need me to come back, I'm only a phone call away."

She reached up and touched his arm where it rested on her shoulder. "Truly, we'll be fine."

He looked doubtful and his next words confirmed the look on his face. "Do you think your *mudder* should look after them again? Just for another day?"

"*Nee.* I'll be fine. Stop fussing."

"She doesn't mind."

"I know, but everything's okay. Stop worrying so much."

He leaned down and kissed her lightly on her forehead. "Shall we go to bed?"

"I might sit up for a while."

"Are you sure?"

"Just a little while."

"Okay." He took his arm away from her shoulders, stood up and then took up the poker, rearranged the fire, and placed on another two logs. "There. That should keep it going until morning." He leaned over and gave her a quick kiss on the lips before he headed upstairs.

Heidi held her head in her hands, wishing that her memory would come back. She couldn't remember their wedding or the births of the children. Surely, they had been the most memorable of days. Then there was the day her father died, and his funeral. She remembered none of it. Nothing.

She closed her eyes tightly and tried her best to

remember everything she'd forgotten. The last memory of Derek was when she was leaving him to become a model in New York. But then she remembered getting on the bus. Was that the point at which her life split into two parallel universes? Two lives running concurrently? If she was in this life, was she also in the other? Who was running her company? It was then that she realized her theory of parallel universes wasn't what was taking place. Janelle didn't even know who she was and if she was living another life in another reality, Janelle would've known who she was.

Going by the theory that if there were two possibilities of something, the most likely explanation was the simpler one, Heidi figured the simplest explanation was that she had lost her memory. The bump on the head had caused something in her brain to trigger a false memory—a detailed memory of another life.

The only thing she could do was to forget that other life she'd thought was real, because it had never existed. She'd never gotten on that bus, she'd never run a successful business and neither did she own a fully paid-off two-million-dollar apartment. It was all a fantasy.

She only wished she didn't feel like such an outsider with her children and her husband. She'd have to get to know him again, and start from scratch with the children. Heidi closed her eyes and asked God for the return of her memory. She wanted to remember those important times in her life, and all those Christmases that had gone out of her head.

CHAPTER 10

Wednesday, December 20

WHEN MICHAEL WOKE up in the middle of the night, Heidi was faced with a dirty diaper, and she realized she was fast running out of clean ones and had forgotten to do the washing the day before. She couldn't believe she wasn't using disposables. Was she really supposed to scrub those dirty diapers? After the diaper change, he had a few mouthfuls of milk and went back to sleep. Heidi crawled back into bed hoping he'd stay asleep because she'd never been able to function without at least eight hours sleep.

She went back to sleep quickly and later woke up to Molly shaking her awake. *"Mamm,* wake up."

She opened her eyes and saw her two girls peering over at her. She vaguely remembered Derek saying goodbye before he left for work. "What is it?"

"It's late. You always wake up when we get up. You said we were going to take *Dat* to *Onkel's* store and then go shopping."

"I completely forgot. I'm sorry." She sat up remembering that Derek said he was going in with Ben today. "We'll have to do it another time if the buggy's not here, but I think it might be. I'm getting up." Heidi knew she had to leave this place. It wasn't her home. She felt like she was being fake and she didn't want to bluff her way through Christmas and have the stress of trying to fool everyone. All she wanted was to be herself and not have to deceive anyone. "Go and wait in the kitchen for me while I get dressed."

The girls turned and walked out of the room. She glanced over at the crib and saw that Michael was still fast asleep. Then, as quickly as that, his legs and arms started moving—he was about to wake up. She thought back to her conversation with Janelle a couple of days ago. Perhaps Janelle was mad at her and was being silly on the phone. Heidi quickly exchanged her cotton nightgown for a dress, and brushed and braided her hair before pinning it under her *kapp*. If all went well, she'd call Janelle again before Michael was fully awake.

As soon as she put her foot on the bottom step, she saw the two girls in the living room. "Didn't I say to wait in the kitchen?"

"We had an accident in the kitchen. Sorry, *Mamm*."

"What do you mean?"

The girls lowered their heads and Heidi hurried into the kitchen. There were broken eggs all over the floor and just about every dish from the cupboard was used and on the countertop.

She looked back at them. "What were you trying to do, exactly?"

"We were making eggs as a surprise."

"Well, it's a surprise all right." She looked down at them and saw their nightgowns had smears of raw egg all over them. "Throw your nighties in the basket and get dressed while I clean up in here."

"Sorry, *Mamm*. Jessica dropped the eggs."

"I couldn't help it. It was an accident."

"It's all right. You had your hearts in the right place. Go up now and get changed and do it quietly, so you don't wake up your *bruder*."

Heidi was disappointed that calling Janelle would have to wait a while now. After she had cleaned the kitchen, she went upstairs to see where her girls were. They were playing in Jessica's room and they were still in their soiled nightgowns. Then Michael cried out. "I told you both to get changed."

"We are."

"*Nee*, you aren't. I can't tell you to do things twice. Once is enough. When you have clean clothes on, come down to the kitchen for your breakfast, and bring these nightgowns with you so I can wash them." When the girls didn't move, she raised her voice. "Do what I said. Now!"

As soon as the girls were on their feet, she hurried to get Michael. She didn't like to hear him cry. Picking him up, she said, "There, that's better." She patted him on the back. "I'll change your diaper and then you can have a nice long bottle."

As she changed him, Jessica appeared by her side.

"Why is he crying like that?" Jessica asked.

"He's hungry of course," Molly answered as she joined her sister in the room, nightgowns in hand.

"I'm glad to see that you're both dressed now. Let's all head downstairs."

Back in the kitchen, Heidi fed Michael his bottle while the girls made toast, since they'd managed to break all the eggs.

When Michael went down for his mid-morning nap, making that phone call popped into Heidi's mind. "You two stay in here where it's warm because I need to make a quick phone call."

"*Jah, Mamm,*" Molly said.

"Watch your *bruder* for me and whatever you do, don't wake him."

Heidi pulled on her thick black coat to shield against the cold and headed out to the shanty that housed the telephone. As soon as she dialed the number, she heard playful screaming coming from behind her. She turned around to see the girls throwing snow at one another and then Jessica fell down flat on her face, and she started crying when Molly picked up a big handful of snow and placed it on her head. Heidi had no choice but to abandon the phone call once more.

"I told you—"

Jessica stood up and then Molly picked up handfuls of snow and started in again, throwing them at Jessica. Jessica screamed again and responded by throwing handfuls of snow back. Heidi could only look on in horror as the girls grew colder in their thin dresses only meant for wearing indoors.

"Inside now, the both of you."

Neither of them moved. Their squeals were so loud that Heidi couldn't even be heard over the top of them.

She grabbed each girl by an arm and marched them inside and closed the door behind her. "Look at you! You're both wringing wet. I told you to stay here and stand by Michael while I went outside."

"Why? He can't go anywhere. He's just a *boppli.*"

"Don't backtalk me, Molly. I've had enough. You're always doing that. Both of you find dry clothes right now, and I'm going to run a hot bath."

"It's too cold for a bath," Jessica said.

"It's not too cold for a bath if you can roll around in the snow."

"We're going," Molly said grabbing her younger sister by the arm.

Heidi checked Michael and saw that he was still asleep, so she headed to the bathroom and let water into the bath. Just as she had finished filling the bath, Michael started crying.

She walked by Molly's room and saw the girls sitting on the bare floor playing with toys. "What did I tell both of you?"

"We're doing it," Jessica said.

"*Nee* you're not. You're playing."

Michael started crying again, louder than before. "You're both likely to get bad colds, and you might even get pneumonia if you don't get in that warm bath right now."

"It's still filling up, I can hear it," Molly said.

"I just turned it off." Heidi was fast losing her patience. "Get your clothes now! And get into the bathroom, now!" Heidi was surprised when she heard herself. She hadn't ever before had reason to scream at anybody. Sure, she felt like screaming at her staff at times, but managed not to. She deliberately lowered her voice and said firmly, "I'm going to get Michael and when I come back I want you both in that bath with your dry clothes ready."

Molly stood. *"Jah, Mamm."*

Jessica stood, too, and the two girls headed for their closets.

Heidi held her screaming baby boy. He was hungry, but she couldn't feed him when she was trying to get her older two children into the bath. They were soaked through to the skin. She caught sight of her reflection in the glass of the living room window. It was a shock to see herself in the Amish clothing, she still wasn't used to it. She didn't want to stay in the community and be Amish, and suffer the constant demands of a family. Was this really her life? Just yesterday she'd thought family life ideal, and now today she was experiencing something close to torture.

"Mamm, Mamm."

The piercing voice of her oldest daughter rang through her head.

"The tap's dripping."

"It'll be fine, it just needs a little fixing. *Dat* can look at it later. Molly, I said to wait in the bathroom with your dry clothes. Do you have dry clothes in there?"

"I can't find any."

"They're in your closet. Where else would they be?"

"There's nothing clean. You haven't washed this week."

"Oh. You and your *schweschder* get into the bath and I'll bring in warm clothes and then after the bath you must sit by the fire to keep warm."

"But, *Mamm.*"

"*Nee!* I've had enough! I told you not to go out in the snow and now look at you. You're dripping wet. If you don't go now and do as I say I'll have a lot to tell your *vadder* when he gets home." She winced when she heard herself say exactly what her own mother used to say to her. When she saw the sour face on Molly, she said, "Lose your attitude and get into that bath NOW!"

Heidi heaved a sigh of relief when Molly turned and headed back up the stairs. She jiggled Michael up and down in an effort to still his cries while she headed to the kitchen to pop his bottle in the hot water to warm.

This wasn't the life for her, it was too hard. Looking after children and changing dirty diapers was such a thankless task. She wanted to get back to her other life, but how could she when she didn't know how she landed back into the Amish life?

She fetched the girls clean nightgowns. They had dresses hanging in their closet like she knew they had, but warm nighties would keep them nice and comfortable. When she got back to the bathroom, she was thankful to see that they were in the warm water.

Once the baby was fed and freshly diapered, and the girls were bathed, dried, dressed, and sitting by the fire,

Heidi took a deep breath and let it out slowly. She had to get back to New York and get back into her life there. If this had been her real life, it wouldn't be so foreign to her. All she had to do was get back to her apartment and her life would be waiting for her.

Heidi crouched down to talk to the girls. "Girls, this time you must listen to me."

They both turned and stared at her. "Stay in the *haus* and look after Michael. I need to make a quick call to someone."

Molly nodded.

She hurried outside and ordered a taxi that would take her to the bus station. Then she hurried back into the house and pulled on her coat, ripped off her prayer *kapp* and threw it over the hook by the door. She could hardly go back to her old life in a *kapp*. Her first stop would be her office where she had a spare set of keys to her apartment.

"Where are we going, *Mamm?*" Molly asked when she saw Heidi her coat.

"I just called a taxi. I'm going somewhere and you're all staying here where you belong."

"You're going without us?" Molly stared at her in disbelief.

"You'll be all right to look after Michael and Jessica until *Dat* gets home, won't you, Molly?" Heidi was certain she was in a dream, so the children would be fine. After all, they didn't really exist except in her mind. "It's only for about half an hour, and you're a big girl now."

"You can't leave us alone, *Mamm*. We're too little," Jessica said.

"Nonsense; you're a big girl now, too." Heidi kneeled down so she would be at eye level with both Molly and Jessica. "The thing is, Molly and Jessica, this is all just a dream. Everything's a dream, all of this. As soon as I walk out the door, you won't be here. You see, you're all in my mind." She clicked her fingers. "All this will be gone."

Molly's eyes opened wide as she blinked at her mother. "Am I having a dream?"

"Me, not you. I'm the one having the dream and you're all in it. You're the *kinner* I would've had if I'd married Derek." She stood up and turned around in a circle. "None of this is real. I need to go back to my real life, and since it hasn't come back to me, I must go back to it."

"Can't we go too?" Jessica asked.

"Don't you see? Don't you both see? None of this is real. You belong here and I belong elsewhere." She stared at her two children who were looking up at her with scrunched faces trying to understand what she was talking about. She crouched down once more thinking what to say. Her best chance of waking up was to find her way back in her dream—find her way back to New York and back to civilization.

"You're scaring me, *Mamm*," Molly said.

When Jessica started to cry, Heidi knew she was stuck there. She couldn't leave these children alone even if they were in her dream and giving her grief.

When the taxi pulled up, she walked outside to send it away. She opened the passenger side door. "I'm sorry but there's been some mistake."

"What do you mean?"

"The taxi was ordered by mistake and we don't need it."

The driver muttered something under his breath.

"Wait. I'll get you some money for your trouble." She figured there had to be some money somewhere in the house. Maybe some kind of housekeeping money, and Molly would know where it was kept.

"Don't bother, lady. I'm never coming back out this way to you people again." He reversed down the driveway.

She headed inside, desperately hoping the children wouldn't say anything to Derek. He was worried enough about her as it was.

CHAPTER 11

ONCE THE TWO girls had settled down and were chattering excitedly to each other about Christmas, Heidi tiptoed out of the room and made herself a hot cup of tea. She came back into the room and was just sitting down on the couch when Jessica ran toward her. "Stop!" Heidi hollered.

Jessica stopped in her tracks and stared at her.

"I've got hot tea here. It could burn you."

Jessica folded her arms and then without warning sat down heavily next to her and Heidi had to lean forward to stop her tea from spilling.

"Just go back and sit with your *schweschder* for a moment. I need just a moment to sit here quietly in silence. And, don't ask me why."

Molly's lips turned down at the corners, and Jessica moved off the couch and sat down next to her sister on the rug. Meanwhile, Michael was making gurgling noises in the crib.

"Someone needs to pick up Michael," Molly said.

"*Nee,* they don't. Not yet. He doesn't have to be picked up all the time as soon as he wakes. Those are his happy sounds. He can be by himself for a moment. Now can I have two minutes of silence, please?"

Both girls turned around and looked at her and then remained quiet.

Never has silence sounded so good, Heidi thought, as she sipped on her hot tea. If this was motherhood, she was ill prepared for it. At least back in her real life, she could close the door of her office or turn her phone off when someone annoyed her. Here, she was trapped.

When she was washing her cup out in the kitchen with one hand and holding Michael on the other hip, she looked out the window hoping the buggy she'd heard was Derek home to help with the children. It wasn't Derek it was her mother.

She heard the children screech from the other room, "It's *Mammi.*"

"Open the door for her and tell her I'm in the kitchen." She sat down and fed the baby while thinking up an excuse. The children were sure to tell her mother that she had nearly gotten into a taxi.

A few minutes later, her mother walked in. "What's this about you going somewhere and leaving the children alone?"

Heidi stared at Jessica and Molly, who were standing either side of *Mamm.* "Go into the other room while I talk to *Mammi.*" The children disappeared into the other room while her mother took a seat at the table. "They were driving me crazy today, and I said something I shouldn't have." She had to admit her wrong. "I did say something about going and leaving them alone."

"You have to rule them with a firmer hand, Heidi. You let them get away with far too much and it results in you getting stressed. It shouldn't go that far and they wouldn't—"

"I know. It's true." She was grateful her mother didn't say she was an awful person. That's exactly what she thought of herself. How could she even consider leaving them alone?

"Give them an inch and they'll take a mile."

"Maybe." Heidi remembered how strict both *Mamm* and *Dat* had been with her when she was growing up. "I'll keep it in mind."

"You need to start early before they become uncontrollable." Her mother looked down at the baby. "How is he today?"

"Good, as usual."

"I hope you learn to do better with him. Why are the girls in their nightgowns already?"

Heidi shook her head. She'd really rather not tell her considering what she'd just said about her parenting. "They were out playing in the snow and it took me ages to get them inside and they had no coats on either. They got soaking wet. I only took my eyes off them for one minute. I managed to get them inside and into a warm bath." Heidi pressed her lips together wondering how those families with more than three children managed. "I didn't know you were coming here today."

"I'm worried about you with that bump on the head you had. Are you sure you're all right? Derek mentioned you were speaking in a weird manner and I didn't notice it at first but he was right, you are speaking in a different way ever since you had that fall."

"That's funny; I feel all right and even the doctor wasn't concerned."

"Well, don't forget I'm not far away if you need help with the *kinner*. Maybe the girls could stay with me for a few days."

"*Nee*, that's fine. I can manage."

"Are you sure?"

Heidi nodded. "Perfectly sure." She wondered where her mother was going to be on Christmas day. Perhaps she was going to join them at Derek's parents'. She didn't ask in case she was already supposed to know.

"Okay, I'll just come right out and say it. I saw you upset when you were at my *haus*. I overheard what the girls said. You didn't even remember *Dat* had died. You had forgotten."

"It's true. I did suffer little bits of memory loss, and at that time I didn't realize that *Dat* had died. It was a weird thing, and it all came back to me in a rush."

"That's a sad thing to have to live over twice."

"*Jah*, it was horrible."

Mamm said, "I miss him a lot. Just because I don't talk about him doesn't mean I don't think about him."

Heidi nodded. "Of course, you were so well matched — well-suited."

"We were. We always knew we'd get married to each other, from when we were very young."

Heidi already knew the story. The community was much smaller back then, and since almost everybody in the community found marriage partners within the group, they grew up with the knowledge they'd most likely marry one another.

"It was all meant to be," Heidi said. "You were the girl next door."

"I was. And then *Gott* needed him home."

"He did." Heidi looked down at her baby to see his eyes closing.

Mamm said, "He sleeps so much. He's either eating or sleeping."

Heidi laughed. "That's what babies do. This one, anyway. Can I make you a hot tea or anything?"

"I had one before I left home. Can I make you one?" Her mother stood up.

"*Nee,* I'm fine."

"And what about the girls? Can I get them some milk and cookies?"

"That would be good. I'm glad you stopped by. You saved me from going out of my mind."

While the girls ate with their grandmother in the kitchen, Heidi put the diapers in the washing machine and then went back to talk with her mother.

When the diapers were washed, Heidi's mother suggested that the best place to dry them was in front of the fire. Her mother helped her get the wooden drying racks from the laundry room and set them up near the fireplace. Then the girls helped them to arrange the diapers on the racks to dry. It might not have looked pretty, but at least they'd dry.

Later, when her mother had gone, she heard Derek come home. Heidi kept the children busy hoping they wouldn't mention to their father that she'd been about to leave them.

The evening passed without the girls opening their mouths about Heidi.

It was right on bedtime when the girls wrapped their arms around her, and then Molly said, "I'm glad you stayed with us, *Mamm*."

"Me too," Jessica said.

Heidi quickly whisked the children upstairs and into their bedrooms hoping Derek hadn't heard what was said.

After she had put the children to bed, tucked them in, and told them to stay put, she headed back down the stairs to Derek, who was sitting quietly reading. She made herself comfortable next to him.

"I've got those gifts ready for the girls."

She sat up straight. "Gifts."

"*Jah*, do you remember?"

"Of course I do."

"Good. I've got all their gifts ready and hidden under a blanket on my workbench. Will you have time to wrap them?"

"*Jah*, I will. *Denke*." He was such a good father and a good husband. She let her back sink into the couch, and looked into the fire. What gifts had they talked about? She was at least pleased that he'd arranged to get them. Finding time in her day to wrap them without the children seeing was an entirely different matter.

WAKING UP WITH A START, Heidi suddenly remembered what she was doing the night before she woke up in the house with Derek. She had fallen asleep while reading her grandmother's travel and recipe diary. Could that diary have had something to do with her being there? It was worth a try, she considered. Tomorrow, she would pay her mother a visit and see if she could borrow the diary that had once belonged to her father's mother, if *Mamm* still had it.

Heidi was still in the living room and Derek was no longer next to her. She glanced at the clock to see it was ten minutes past twelve. With her new plan giving her hope, she sat upright, folded the crocheted blanket and placed it over the back of the couch, and then crept quietly up the stairs.

CHAPTER 12

Thursday, December 21

THE NEXT MORNING, Heidi woke to see Derek pulling on his coat. He was fully dressed and even had on his hat.

"I've got to leave now," he whispered when he glanced at her and saw her eyes open. "The children are still asleep and I've made a bottle for Michael. It just needs heating when he wakes."

"Okay *denke.*"

"Ben's picking me up, so you can use the buggy."

"*Denke.*"

He gave her a quick kiss on her forehead, then left the room. Derek was such a gentle kind man and being with him seemed so right. So much so that she didn't like keeping her other life a secret from him, but she had to. If only she'd met him in New York and he wasn't an Amish man. Things could've been so different for them.

Wanting to make an early start to get her hands on Agnes's diary, she got dressed and headed downstairs to prepare the children's breakfast. After Molly and Jessica appeared in the kitchen, Michael cried out from his crib in the bedroom.

"There's your *bruder* awake now."

"I'll get him." Molly raced toward the stairs.

"*Nee.* You're too small to carry him, and you're certainly not going to carry him down the stairs. Go sit with your *schweschder* in the kitchen."

Molly turned around and with downturned lips, said, "Can I give him his bottle?"

"*Jah*, you can do that. If you sit upright on the couch, hold him carefully and don't move."

When Heidi reached the crib, Michael was crying hard. "Oh, baby, don't cry." Once he was in her arms, he stopped crying. She gave him a quick kiss and then changed his diaper. "*Dat* could at least have done this before he left this morning." She giggled. "Wake him up before he leaves next time, would you?"

Once she was back in the kitchen, she warmed the bottle and then walked back into the living room. She placed Michael on Molly's lap with his bottle. "Keep still. No moving about."

"I know how to do it, *Mamm.*"

Heidi sat next to her ready to grab the baby if he fell.

"Can I have a hold next?" Jessica asked, peering over Molly's shoulder.

"Maybe when you're a little bigger. Today we're going to *Mammi's haus.*"

"Again? We were there only the other night," Molly said.

"*Jah* again. There was something I forgot to collect while I was there."

"What is it?" asked Molly.

"It's something very special that belonged to my *Dat's mudder.*" Knowing she'd only be asked further questions, she added, "It's a book, something like a diary. It has recipes in it and stories of her travels she made when she was a young woman."

"How young, *Mamm?* Can you please tell me?" Jessica asked.

"A lot older than you."

"*Denke, Mamm,*" Jessica said.

"I'll take the *boppli* now, Molly, so you can eat at the kitchen table. Come on, let's go."

Once Heidi had the baby at the breakfast table, she held the baby in one arm while she ate breakfast with her other hand.

"Tell us more about the book, *Mamm,*" Jessica asked pushing back her light brown hair.

"It was before she was married that she made all the entries in it. I guess she was about sixteen. No, she would have had to be older than that to travel around by herself. She must've been eighteen or even twenty. *Jah,* I think about twenty."

"That's old," Jessica said.

"Do you want it because you want to show it to us, *Mamm?*" Molly asked.

"I'll show it to you if *Mammi* will allow me to borrow it."

"She will. She's kind like that." Jessica said, sitting down cross-legged on the floor.

"Move onto the rug, Jessica."

Jessica scooted over to the rug. A twinge of guilt ran through Heidi. She only wanted the book in the hope she'd be taken back to her other life, but that meant leaving the children behind when she was just getting to know them. Molly was the strong-willed one, that was quite plain to see. Jessica was gentler and was always careful to say please and thank you.

Heidi looked down at the baby in her arms. Michael had a good temperament and only cried when he needed feeding or changing. Something told Heidi that his good nature would be an advantage to him when he got older, with his two older sisters around. She was certain when he grew a little older, Molly would force him to play her games of make-believe, whether he liked it or not.

When the washing up was done and the girls fully dressed, Heidi propped the baby on the couch and left the two girls in charge while she headed outside to hitch the buggy. Soon they were on their way to her mother's house, and since she didn't know how to work the buggy heater, they were wrapped in blankets to keep out the cold.

Mornings in Lancaster County were so different from mornings in the city. The air was fresh and clean and there was not a person to be seen. A far cry from the crowded streets, police sirens, and car horns of New York City.

"I'm so cold. I can't wait to get to *Mammi's haus* and I hope she's got the fire roaring," Jessica said.

"She always does, even when it's not cold," Molly said.

Heidi glanced down at Molly. "Cover yourself with the blanket more."

"Nee, I'm not cold. I don't need to."

"Really? You're not cold?"

"Nee."

Heidi recalled she'd been like that when she was a child. Everyone tried to force coats on her and she was always saying she wasn't cold. It seemed some young children didn't feel the cold as much as adults.

"I can see the smoke coming out of *Mammi's* chimney," Jessica squealed.

"Me too," Molly said. "And I saw it first."

"I did. Didn't I, *Mamm?"*

"I don't know who saw it first, I'm just glad *Mammi* feels the cold because I'm freezing."

As soon as she pulled up the horse, the two girls climbed down and ran to knock on their grandmother's door.

"Only one of you need knock," Heidi called out as she picked up the baby. "Otherwise, you'll drive *Mammi* crazy."

"Is *Mammi* crazy?" Jessica asked just as Heidi's mother opened the door.

Her mother looked over at Heidi. "I'm crazy, am I? Is that what you think?"

As Heidi walked to the house, she was pleased to see her mother was smiling. The two girls were already inside. "I said their constant knocking would make you crazy. It sure would make me crazy."

"It did give me a fright. Come in out of the cold."

Once they were all sitting around the fire with hot chocolate, Heidi figured she better get to the point of why they were there. "Do you remember that old book of Agnes's?"

"Nee. What book?"

Heidi's heart sank. "She wrote it when she was a young girl. *Dat* showed it to me once. It has recipes and she wrote about her travels that she went on when she was young, before she married."

Lines deepened in *Mamm's* forehead and she slowly shook her head. "I can't recall anything like that."

"Don't you?"

"Nee. I've got an old box of things of your *vadder's* in the spare room, though, if you'd like to have a look through those."

"Could I?"

"Of course. Help yourself."

Heidi smiled and passed her baby over to her mother. "You girls stay here a moment, I won't be long." Heidi walked away trying not to appear too anxious, and trying not to get her hopes up. This book might help her cross the portal back to her other life. That's the only thing she had done differently that night apart from praying. The book was her only hope and that didn't mean that God didn't have a hand in it all. Maybe it was God who had reminded her of the diary last night.

She found the box in the closet and dragged it out. Sitting down next to it she started pulling things out. It was filled with old letters and yellowed newspaper clippings. Then, at the bottom of the box, she found it. It looked just the same as the day *Dat* gave it to her. She remembered it was Christmas Eve. Everyone had tried to talk her into staying at least until after Christmas, but she knew if she stayed another Christmas, she might never leave.

She placed the book carefully on the bed and then put the box back in the closet.

"Is that it? You found it?" her mother asked when Heidi walked down the stairs.

"This is it."

Mamm held out her hand. "Give me a look."

She sat back down next to her mother, with Michael now asleep on the couch between them, and handed the diary over.

"I honestly don't remember ever seeing this. When did your *vadder* show it to you?"

"It would have to have been ten years ago or more. Do you mind if I borrow it?"

"Suit yourself." *Mamm* handed it back. "Keep it if you want. I probably would've gotten rid of that old box anyway when I got around to it. They're mostly letters from people I don't know; people your *vadder* knew before he met me." Her mother took back the book and flipped through the pages. "She certainly did travel to a lot of places."

"*Jah*, I forgot about the book until the other day."

"Maybe that fall you had jogged your memory? You remembered some things and forgot some things."

Heidi nodded. "*Jah*, that must be it."

Her mother handed back the book once more, and then turned her attention to the girls. "Would you two like to help me make some cookies?"

The girl's faces lit up.

"Could we, *Mamm*?" Molly asked.

Heidi's mother stared at her. "Is that all right? Do you have the time to spare?"

She nodded. "Of course. That sounds like a lot of fun."

"You stay here with the *boppli, Mamm,* and we'll help *Mammi,* all right?" Jessica asked.

"Okay, if that's okay with *Mammi,* I don't mind staying by the fire."

Her mother said to Jessica, "You don't want *Mamm* to help us?"

"We can do it by ourselves with you."

"Let's do it," Molly said.

The three of them headed to the kitchen, leaving Heidi alone with the baby. She studied the book in her lap and made up a plan. Tonight, she would do exactly what she had done the last night she was in her apartment and that was take the book to bed with her and read it until she fell asleep.

She studied Agnes's handwriting. It was so even and beautiful, with careful scrolls on the capital letters. She looked at the recipes for Christmas cookies and just as she'd thought, it was the same recipe as the one that had been in her head when she and the girls had made star cookies. It confused her that her *Mamm* had forgotten about the book. It was the one thing *Dat* had from his side of the family.

Heidi closed her eyes, trying to remember everything she'd been told about her father's mother. She had died when Heidi was only six months old and thus Heidi had no memory of her. Agnes had married and had three sons, of whom her father was the eldest. According to her father, his mother's parents, Greta and John, had been conservative and it was odd that they had permitted Agnes to travel about by herself. It was unusual for a young Amish woman to travel alone.

Agnes had only traveled from community to community, so she couldn't have gotten herself into too much trouble. Heidi wondered if Agnes had been resented by her siblings. Often the youngest one in the family was spoiled and was resented by the older ones. Being an only child, Heidi hadn't experienced this.

Heidi looked down at Michael and wondered if the girls would resent him. She figured they probably wouldn't because he was a boy. He opened his eyes and looked at her and she couldn't stop the smile that covered her face. Could she really leave him? Somehow, he didn't feel like he was her baby, but she couldn't deny the feeling that gnawed inside her that these three children needed her.

Knowing he'd soon be crying from hunger, she picked him up and headed to the kitchen to heat his bottle. The girls were standing by the table as *Mamm* was showing them how to measure things correctly.

"*Mamm* has a recipe in her head," Molly told her grandmother.

"We all have recipes for different things in our heads. You will too when you get older."

Molly's eyes bugged open.

"I love cooking," Jessica said. "I especially love cooking cookies."

"That might have something to do with you liking to eat them," Heidi's mother said.

Molly and Jessica giggled.

"I like eating them too. They're my favorite food. What's your favorite food, *Mammi?*"

"Less talking and more concentrating on what you're doing, Molly, or you'll never learn what I'm teaching you."

Heidi felt a little sorry for Molly when she heard her mother's stern tone; that was how she'd been raised and her mother was probably raised even more strictly, with even more of a no-nonsense approach.

Once the bottle was heated, Heidi sat down at the kitchen table and fed Michael while she watched the girls cutting out the cookie dough with different shaped cutters. She had loved doing the same when she was a girl, and she'd especially loved eating the leftovers on the sides of the mixing bowl.

CHAPTER 13

THAT NIGHT, Heidi had everything organized in her mind. After the children had been put to bed, she gave them special kisses and said goodnight while thinking goodbye. Then she sat by the fire with Derek, and when he went to bed, she told him she wouldn't be far behind him.

As soon as her husband was up the stairs, she pulled out the diary from underneath the couch where she'd hidden it.

Please take me back, book, if you have some secret powers. What am I talking about? God has done this to show me the other road I could've taken. God, thank you for showing me what could've been. I'd like to go home now. Amen.

She found the part where she'd fallen asleep back in the apartment, covered herself in a blanket, took a last look around her home, and then settled back to read more of her grandmother's adventures.

TODAY I WAS AMAZED to see a familiar face arrive at Aunt Elsie's farm. It was Malachi Arnold. He's always at our place and my parents think highly of him. Sally Anne seemed too pleased to see him and now she won't stop talking about him. She wouldn't stop talking to him and no one else could get a word out, and that annoyed me more than a little. She kept looking at him from under her eyelashes with her head tilted in a funny way. I'm sure she thought she looked adorable as she smiled at him. I hoped he didn't think so. He didn't seem to pay her any mind. No more than anyone else if you deduct all the time she was talking. I mean, he had to look at her when she was speaking. It would've been rude not to.

I heard her whisper to her mother, "He's so tall and handsome."

"He's too old for you, Sally Anne. He must be nearly thirty," Aunt Elsie told her.

"That's fine by me," replied Sally Anne. "With looks like that who cares how old he is?"

My instincts were right. Sally Anne likes him. I hope he doesn't marry her and move away from our community. Mamm and Dat would be most upset if that happened. They enjoy having him to the house.

NOW IT IS the next night and we had another of Mammi's recipes. Mammi is Mamm's and Aunt Elsie's mudder, but I'm sure Mamm doesn't have all these recipes. I spooned into my mouth a dish called family beef potato pie. I helped her cook it. It was baked in a deep dish with layers of ground beef and chopped onion, mashed potato, and grated cheese, and then topped with loads more potato and baked until it was golden brown. It was really *good! Aunt Elsie says she sometimes adds vegetables, too, such as peas and corn and carrots.*

Family Beef and Potato Pie
Ingredients:
3 pounds ground beef
1 large onion, chopped
¼ cup flour
2-3 cups beef broth or water
1 pound cheese, grated
5 pounds potatoes, boiled and mashed in advance
salt and pepper to taste
optional – peas, corn, lightly cooked chopped carrots, about 2 pounds total.
Cookware
Large frying pan
Large deep casserole dish

Method
Heat oven to 325 F
Brown beef and onion in frying pan, adding salt and pepper if desired.
Stir flour into juices in frying pan, mixing until smooth. Add broth or water slowly, stirring constantly to make a thick gravy.
Layer into casserole as follows:
1/3 of the meat mixture
½ of vegetables (if using them)
½ of cheese

¼ of mashed potatoes

Repeat above layers, then all remaining meat.

Remaining mashed potatoes as top crust, covering to edges of the dish.

Bake until bubbling-hot throughout and top of mashed potatoes is browned. (About 1 hour).

EVERYONE GAVE *thanks for the food before we ate and Aunt Elsie told Malachi that I made the food. She made it sound like I made it by myself and I could tell Sally Anne didn't like what her mother said. Her face didn't show she was annoyed, but I could feel it because the tension filled the air.*

Again, Sally Anne tried to make me look silly. This is what she said, "Agnes was sent to learn to cook and sew, Malachi. Can you believe that at her age?" Then Sally Anne gave me a little smirk while Malachi finished chewing his mouthful.

"Don't worry, Sally Anne," I said, "I'm a fast learner." Then I gave her a sweet smile to let her know she hadn't upset me in front of everyone. I should've said something clever, but I didn't know what else to say.

"Agnes's mudder is a gut cook and don't the dochders learn from their mudders?" Malachi asked.

"Jah, but she can't do it." Sally Anne laughed.

I felt I had to explain myself. "Amy, my schweschder, and Mamm get so involved they tend to leave me out, but with Amy getting married soon, Mamm will have time to show me everything."

Malachi smiled at me. I think he felt sorry for me, the way I had to explain my lack of cooking skills in front of everyone at the table.

Sally Anne leaned over the table and touched Malachi lightly on his hand, in a desperate way. "Malachi, can I show you around the farm tomorrow?" Her voice irritated me, and she kept talking before he had a chance to respond. "We have milking cows, pigs, chickens, turkeys, farm horses and we grow all our own fruit and vegetables."

My uncle said to her, "Sorry Sally Anne, Malachi is here just a few days, and he is riding with me to the high country tomorrow. I want his advice on some extra farm equipment I'm thinking of purchasing."

Sally Anne pouted.

Aunt Elsie said, "Before Malachi leaves, we'll all go on horse-back and have a picnic by the river."

I can say I was more than a little shocked that Aunt Elsie suggested to go horseback riding. My mudder would say that was worldly and like an Englisch sport. Then I remembered each community has a slightly different Ordnung. I would probably see and hear many things like this on my travels.

It cheered Sally Anne up when she heard about the picnic, because she announced loudly, "I will do all the cooking for the picnic."

"Nee," said her mother. "I want Agnes to do it."

With that, Sally Anne stood and left the room even before dessert and with food still on her plate. No one at the table said anything for a while. Everyone was shocked at her sudden departure. If she thinks Malachi would like someone who does things like that, she's mistaken. She has a temper, she must have, to do something like that. I know she likes Malachi, and doesn't like me, but I've done nothing to her.

Perhaps she doesn't like having visitors staying in the house. It seemed much like a small child's temper tantrum, and I thought I would not like to be Sally Anne later, when her father spoke to her about it.

I've been busy and tired, so I've missed writing for a couple of days. Now it is Thursday morning, and things have not improved with Sally Anne. I tried to be nice and then I gave up and now I altogether avoid her. Nothing I do or say pleases her and she's always finding fault when I help with the cooking. I suppose that's good because I need to learn what I'm doing wrong and I shouldn't let her annoy me so.

Today is the day of the picnic. I am up and dressed very early. Yesterday, I helped Aunt Elsie with the food for the picnic. We made roast chickens, and cake, as well as some small apple pies. I hope today will be enjoyable. I'm not used to horseback riding, but I found out that around here they do it quite a bit. Aunt Elsie said after breakfast we'll make sandwiches and then be on our way.

Now it is night time and the picnic was enjoyable. I have a sore bottom from riding the horse and sore lips from the dry wind. We must've been riding for two hours, and after our picnic it was another two hours back. The day was more about the riding than the picnic, I am guessing, otherwise, why go so far away for a picnic?

It was nice where we had the picnic. It was by a fast-running river, and we tied the horses up in the shade where they had lots of grass. Aunt Elsie spread out a large blanket and we all helped her place the food in the middle. Sally Anne deliberately waited until Malachi sat down and then she sat next to him. I sat on the edge of the blanket facing half away from everyone. Onkel Robert talked

134

a lot about farming to Malachi and I wondered if he was talking so much so Sally Anne wouldn't get a word in.

Sally Anne then came and sat beside me and asked me why I was so upset. She said it loud enough for everyone to hear. I insisted I wasn't upset, I was merely enjoying Gott's handiwork in the beauty surrounding us. She looked shocked at my response.

While we were there at the picnic, Aunt Elsie told me I'll be leaving soon and be onto my next adventure. The next place is only twenty miles away. Onkel Robert is taking me halfway to meet the next people I'm staying with. I am to leave the day after tomorrow. Tomorrow, Aunt Elsie said she has some more things to show me in the kitchen before I leave.

Sally Anne added that I have much more to learn and I smiled and thanked her and Aunt Elsie for showing me so many cooking skills and sharing so many lovely recipes.

We only just finished the food and Onkel Robert said we should head back. I wasn't ready to leave because I just wanted to sit awhile. Maybe I'd been sitting incorrectly on the horse as no one else seemed to be troubled by a sore rear. I found more pleasure in sitting on the blanket than I had riding the horse and I wasn't pleased to have another two hours of it on the way back. At least it's over and I won't have to do it again.

THIS IS my last night at Aunt Elsie's farm. After breakfast, Malachi came to say goodbye. He added he might see me again before I finally arrive home. I figured that meant he knew where I was going on my journey and he might be at one of the upcoming places too. After I said goodbye, I told him it was nice that he'd been there. He looked a little shocked that I said that, but I think he was also pleased. It was a little hard to tell.

Aunt Elsie sat me down at the kitchen table to give me advice on keeping a house. The first advice she gave me was to always bake enough bread. She said she'd give me more breadmaking practise that day and she did. Then she told me to always have cookies and cake on hand in case visitors stop by.

Before I went to bed tonight, she told me she'd loved having me here. She must really like me because she said it's a pity we live so far from each other. Then she told me I learn fast and my parents will be pleased when she writes to tell them about my visit. Then she said something that shocked me. This is what she said, "I think Malachi has feelings for you. I see the way he looks at you."

I shook my head. "We're just friends," I insisted. Secretly, I was pleased with what she said about Malachi. I've never had a man like me and I think I'm starting to like him. He's quiet, but he's thoughtful and kind.

I will write more after I arrive at Mr. and Mrs. Jemison's place tomorrow.

HERE I AM at the Jemison's horse-breeding farm in Youngstown and it's very late at night. The home is another large log cabin type of home, and it is a family farm but mainly for horse breeding. There are two or three cows for milking and some chickens, a large vegetable garden and some apple trees. Mr. and Mrs. Jemison once lived in our community until they married and moved to this property years ago. It was left to Mr. Jemison by his uncle.

The Jemisons have three sons. Job, Jeremiah, and Abraham. All are in their twenties and not married. There probably aren't enough women here for them. Mr. and Mrs. Jemison asked me to call them Aunt Sarah and Onkel Abel. Aunt Sarah is a short motherly woman with an ample bosom. When we were alone, she told me all the women in her family are short and fat. She used the word 'squat,' which I suppose sounds a little better.

When Mrs. Jemison saw me for the first time, she said, "You are a dear little girl, so pretty and delicate. We will have to fatten you up. You are too thin."

I didn't tell her I was not intending to fatten myself up. I'm not even skinny, I'm just normal and average size, aside from being short. The way I am is just normal for me, just as she is naturally squat. I asked if I could help her cook while I was here and she seemed pleased and then she told me she wrote Mamm that she would give me all her cooking secrets.

I was so pleased and thanked her. I know it's a big thing for women to hand over their cooking secrets. Aunt Sarah told me that making good food and being a hardworker was a way to a man's heart. I nearly laughed, but stopped myself because she hadn't meant it to be funny. I think she could see I was about to laugh because she shot me a funny look and her icy blue eyes fixed themselves upon me. I had to look away from her.

Then she told me to read Proverbs 31 about a virtuous woman. I told her I would and that I brought a bible with me from home. I could tell she was pleased about that and she gave me a big smile.

For the evening meal tonight, we had roast beef, roasted corn on the cob, sweet potatoes and beets, with fresh crusty bread to soak up the extra gravy. Dessert was a lemon meringue pie with cream. I found out I love lemon meringue pie and it could very well be my newest favorite dessert. I could eat dessert and nothing else. That would be good, I thought, if I never ate meat and vegetables again and then had room for more dessert. I could eat three or four desserts at one time.

· · ·

BEFORE DINNER, I met the Jemison boys. Job, the eldest was short like his mother, and fairly plain in the looks department. Jeremiah was tall, slim and very good-looking, like his father would've been in his youth. Abraham was not very good-looking, and neither did he look like either of his parents. Although, he did have lovely dark curly hair and a friendly smile.

After the dinner and the washing up was done, both Aunt Sarah and I joined the men in the living room in front of a huge fire. It wasn't even very cold outside. At home, we wouldn't have had the fire on in this hot weather. It seemed like a big waste of firewood to me. Not just the wood but the time and the effort to cut all the wood. I guess with three big men in the house, four including Onkel Abel, it wouldn't be such an effort for them. It seemed a waste to me, and Mamm would've thought the same.

Jeremiah said to me, "What are you doing here, Agnes? Surely such a pretty woman as you could find plenty of suitable men for choosing a husband where you came from. It's such a large community."

That shocked Aunt Sarah. "Jeremiah? Enough!"

It was then that I realized everyone would think I was traveling to find a husband. "Maybe I'm not interested in marriage." I don't know why I said it, but the moment I did, I regretted it as everyone gasped. I'd shocked all of them.

Job, the eldest spoke up with a stern voice, and said, "Gott made woman and He made man to marry and have kinner, and the sooner you learn that, the better for you."

I nodded. What else could I do? I didn't want to say that Gott didn't make man and woman for only that purpose. I mean, who knows the mind of Gott? After this, there was an awkward silence. Aunt Sarah asked if I would like an early night and, after that business, I was eager to agree to one. I wonder if they want *to send me right back home? Or, maybe on to my next place early?*

In future, I will keep out of Job's way and think before I speak. I didn't like Job's beady little eyes judging me.

Now it is *the next night. They didn't send me away after that awful exchange with Job. I've managed to stay in the kitchen all day and learn some of Aunt Sarah's secrets. She's always telling me things from the bible and quoting things.*

I asked her for the recipe to the lemon meringue pie. She gave it to me to copy out right then, and tonight I will copy it again, right here in my book in case I lose the paper I wrote it on.

∽

Lemon Meringue Pie
First you'll need to bake the pastry.
Sweet Pie Cookie-style Pastry:
Ingredients:
½ cup butter
½ cup sugar
2 cups flour
1 egg

METHOD:
Cream the butter and the sugar.
Add egg and beat well
Add sifted flour.
Knead lightly

Roll out to size and press into pie tin.

Bake in a moderate oven for about twenty minutes, until lightly browned.

Set on a rack to cool.

FILLING:

Ingredients:

2 tablespoons of plain flour

2 tablespoons of cornflour (cornstarch)

Half a cup of white sugar

Half a cup of lemon juice

Half a cup of boiling water

Two egg yolks

Grated outer-layer of one lemon (the "zest")

1 tablespoon butter

MERINGUE:

2 egg whites

4 tablespoons of sugar

METHOD:

Blend flour, cornflour and sugar in a saucepan with water along with the lemon juice. Bring to a boil while stirring constantly.

Boil until it thickens and keep stirring.

Add lightly- beaten egg yolks, butter and lemon rind, and stir until mixed well.

Place in already baked and cooled pie crust.

. . .

BEAT EGG WHITES until stiff

Add sugar gradually and continue beating until thick.

Pile on top of pie and place in a very moderate oven or under a slow griller until lightly brown.

TODAY I also learned how to make apple pie and custard. Aunt Sarah didn't cook it, she just told me how she makes it and allowed me to copy the recipe out. She said her pie crust for the apple pie is different from others and she makes it with crushed cookies. That's her big secret. She also has a secret for preparing the apples for the pie.

The secret she told me is that she drains all the liquid from the apples by heating them, straining them, letting them stand until they have cooled, and then heating them slightly again to take out all the liquid and letting them cool again. It seems a lot of trouble, but she assures me that it really does make a difference.

I'm not just going to take her say-so on it. The first time, I'm going to try what she said to do, and then the next time, I'm just going to strain the stewed apple once and then I'll compare the results. I hope the shorter way tastes as good.

Tomorrow night we are having turkey and vegetables. It's a plain dish and I don't know if I'll learn much from that. It's just putting a turkey in the oven and then baking the vegetables. Even I can do that.

I also heard that Malachi Arnold will be arriving for dinner and staying here until I leave for Mamm's cousin's house in Munfordville. He's not staying here in this house, but here with someone else in the community. Elizabeth, Mamm's cousin, has a store and is famous for her jams, pickles, and chutneys. Mamm has always talked a lot about her and I can't wait to meet her.

Aunt Sarah says I'll be an expert cook by the time I arrive home and I'll be ready to make some man a gut fraa. She even said if I strive hard, I might become a virtuous woman. I wonder if she judges herself as a virtuous woman. Most likely or she wouldn't say I might become one.

Then she said, "Don't overlook my boys. I can see Jeremiah has taken a liking for you, but he is greatly influenced by his vadder *and his* bruder. *They are both trying to persuade him to marry Betty Mueller. She is strong and solid like me and would make an excellent choice for him."*

"Why is Malachi Arnold coming here?" I asked, ignoring what she said about Jeremiah. She didn't seem to mind that I didn't comment about Jeremiah.

"I believe he wants to purchase some of our horses. He's coming from such a long way because he has heard how good they are."

I didn't believe it. We shall see if he buys any of their horses. Even if he did, how would he get them home? It's such a distance from where we live and we don't have trouble buying horses in our community. There are plenty of them. I'm starting to think that Malachi Arnold is Mamm's secret plan. It is most likely a match-making plan and if that is so, it's deeply embarrassing.

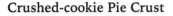

Crushed-cookie Pie Crust
Ingredients:
2 cups crushed cookies
½ cup melted butter

⅓ cup sugar
Method:
Mix all the ingredients together and press evenly onto the base and sides of the pie dish
Bake in a moderately high oven for ten minutes.

HEIDI YAWNED, and was too tired to read more. Did Agnes end up marrying Malachi? Was that Agnes's mother's secret plan? *Dat* never talked about his history or his family. Heidi didn't even know her own paternal grandmother's name until she was given the diary. Heidi was tempted to skip to the end and hopefully there'd be a proper conclusion to what happened to Agnes. Going by the size of the diary, it seemed possible. She hugged the diary to herself and closed her eyes.

CHAPTER 14

Friday, December 22

HEIDI WOKE up to glaring sunlight. She shaded her eyes and then realized she'd fallen asleep on the couch. But it wasn't the couch in her Amish home. She jumped to her feet and looked around. She was delighted to be back in her New York apartment. Hearing a thud, she looked down to see her grandmother's diary had landed on the floor. She looked down at it and moved it out of the way with her foot.

She excitedly ran around the apartment and then stopped at the mirror in the bathroom. There were dark circles under her eyes and she looked pale and tired, but her hair was back to the short style, and because she'd been sleeping it was sticking out on end. She turned on the tap, wet her hands, and smoothed down her hair.

On hearing the traffic in the street below, she ran to

the living room window and opened it. There were cars and crowds, smog and noise. *Yes!* This was her real life and she was back!

She pulled her iPhone out of her handbag in the bedroom to see it was December 22, Friday, at six in the morning. This was the day of the staff Christmas party. It can't have been a dream because she'd lost days—as many days as she'd lived with Derek.

Whatever had happened, she was pleased to be back. "I'm back!"

When she walked to the couch, she picked up her grandmother's diary.

"Thank you, and *denke,* Grandmamma." She never wanted to leave again. It was nice to have lived something that might've been, but even better to be back home. Never again did she want to go back to the confines of the restrictive Amish community. She had a taste of what her life would've been like if she'd stayed and married Derek and it would've been exhausting married to Derek with three children. There were too many constant demands and way too many menial tasks. It was much easier to deal with the infighting of the realtors squabbling over commissions and leads.

She smiled when she looked down and saw that she was wearing a silky cream robe. No longer would she have to wear those dreadful Amish clothes that covered her from head to foot and showed nothing of her figure.

What had happened in this life while she was gone? That was something she wasn't sure she wanted to know. It was all too much to handle and to think about. She raced to the bathroom again and had a quick shower, enjoying the fact that she didn't have to worry about getting her long hair wet.

After her shower, she changed into her usual attire of tight-fitting skirt and blouse, and the jacket that matched the skirt. Once she'd applied make-up and slipped on a pair of dressy heels, she grabbed her bag and overcoat, and headed to her regular café for breakfast.

As soon as she stepped through the door, it concerned her that the café had changed. If the café was different, what else would be different back here in this life? She felt a little comforted when Ralph, the owner of the café, saw her and waved. After she had waved back, she walked to her usual table, noticing that instead of carpet there were polished floorboards. Patterned graffiti wallpaper adorned the walls, and black steel pendant lights hung from the ceiling.

She slid into her usual booth at the back of the café. She was glad that it was free and they still had the same familiar arrangement of tables within the four walls. After she had pulled her laptop out of her bag, she resumed work on her speech for the Christmas party.

She caught the owner's attention and he walked over. "What's happened here, Ralph?"

He chuckled. "You didn't notice the work going on over the last couple of days?"

"I've been away."

"I should've told you, but we did have a sign on the door that we'd be undergoing the renovations. We've been closed for the last few days."

Heidi shook her head. "I didn't notice the sign."

"Didn't you? It was up for several weeks."

"I don't usually notice things like that. It looks good, though."

"Thanks. We're all finished. This is the first day of the new look. I'm pleased you like it."

"It's very on trend."

"Thanks. I better get back to making your coffee."

She turned back to her laptop and kept working on her speech. She always made one right before she gave out the bonuses, a clever trick to make certain that all her staff attended. Although, the free food and alcohol might have been enough to ensure that. The staff party was another opportunity to motivate her workers. They too could be as successful as she, if they worked smart and if they worked hard. She'd inspire them by once again telling them her story of how she got to where she was from nothing.

"Here you go, Heidi. One cheese and ham croissant and a double shot cappuccino."

"Thanks, Ralph."

The owner of the café placed her food down in front of her.

After she stared at the chocolate sprinkles on the froth, she was reminded that Derek had thought she liked a totally different kind of coffee. There was an emptiness within, a sensation of emptiness without Derek. Her heart was like a desert wasteland. She dismissed the feeling as quickly as it had come, took a sip of coffee, and then took a bite of her croissant while telling herself how good it was to be back home where she belonged, in her familiar surroundings. Nearly every day she had breakfast at that café. The only exceptions were when she had morning staff meetings in the boardroom where fresh pastries and coffee were served.

After Heidi spent some time on her speech, she thought more about her goals. Sure, she'd come a long way, but she wanted to reach higher. There was a need for her kind of business all across the country, in every city of any size. Before she opened more offices, though, she had to get this office and her staff running smoothly. Right now, she had to focus on getting through Christmas.

She finished her croissant and wiped her fingers on a paper napkin. In the new year, she'd eat better and start going to a gym. After she did some more work on her speech, she jotted down some ideas for new year's resolutions. Some of her ideas were to get new friends, people who didn't work for her, and to find time to travel.

Once she was finished, she packed her computer away, drained the last of her coffee, which was now cold, and then headed out of the café. Her office was only a five-minute walk from the coffee shop.

CHAPTER 15

HEIDI WALKED into her office and was pleased to see Lee's smiling face looking at her from behind the reception desk. The other receptionist was busy taking a call.

"Good morning, Lee. Any messages for me?"

"Yes, I emailed them all to you."

"Thanks." She leaned against the counter. "How are we doing with the situation regarding the leads? Any more complaints?"

Lee rolled her eyes. "There are always complaints. No one's happy."

"I'm fine tuning a few solutions."

Lee nodded. "That would be good. They keep blaming me."

"Just keep doing what you're doing, for the moment."

"I will."

Heidi gave her a smile and kept walking through to her office. Lee wasn't stupid, she knew to give Janelle the expensive leads because she was reliable and closed the highest percentage. She pushed the door of her office open and sat behind her highly polished wooden desk. Then she looked up at the awards she and her agency had won. When she first started working in real estate, someone said to her, *'you're only as good as your last sale,'* and she found that could be applied to everything in life. If you're not moving ahead, you're falling behind.

Her assistant, Amanda, knocked on her door.

"Come in."

"Heidi, I just got the final numbers for the party tonight."

"We should've had them days ago."

"We did, but a couple more people are coming. It shouldn't make too much difference."

"Okay, call them through to Jill." Jill was the caterer. She'd been catering their Christmas parties for the last five years.

When Amanda left, from the security camera monitor in her office, Heidi saw the sales staff coming through the door just before nine. She clicked on her desktop computer and looked in her diary to see what appointments she had. She had a meeting with Frank Dyson, a successful and well-known developer. He had several apartments he couldn't sell and was thinking of leasing them. After that, the only thing she had was the party at six. It was going to be an easy day, and if she landed Frank's business ... she'd only need one appointment like that a day to keep her well ahead of the game.

Then Heidi clicked over to have a look at the various appointments that the agents had booked. When she saw the bright blue bars across all the timelines, she put her hands behind her head and leaned back. Each of her agents had at least four office-generated appointments.

She was so pleased to be back in her normal life where she felt comfortable. She didn't have to pretend to be anybody she wasn't. Motherhood was something she'd thought she wanted at some stage, but experiencing how hard it was had given her second thoughts.

Just to see what kind of office space was out there, she turned back to her computer and scrolled through the commercial listings. She sent off a couple of emails when she saw two places she liked. Ten minutes later, she got a text with an agent offering to show her one of the office suites. She agreed, even though the time he had chosen to show it to her was on Sunday, and that was Christmas Eve.

IT HAD BEEN a surprise to hear from Frank Dyson. She'd sold apartments for him back when she was selling real estate rather than handling rentals. She'd always gotten along well with him. Heidi had dropped the ball regarding Frank. She should've kept in contact with him as she had done with all her other developers, but the few times she had approached him about leasing out his unsold apartments, he hadn't been interested in even talking it over.

Before her appointment with him, she'd studied his two latest projects. They weren't selling, and now was her chance to sell him on her agency. She would have to mention that their aim was to find their clients a perfect apartment in one day, along with naming all the other advantages of using her agency. They were the top leasing agency in New York.

She made sure she got to the bar early and was sipping iced water through a straw when she heard his loud voice. When she looked up she saw him with his phone up to his ear as he walked toward the table. He wore a dark blue long-sleeved shirt and gray pants. The shirt was unbuttoned way too far and a heavy gold chain hung around his neck. She gave him a little wave and he smiled at her and promptly finished his conversation. Just as she stood and reached out her hand, he leaned over and kissed her on both cheeks. He needed a closer shave; his whiskers were rough against her cheeks, and his face was sweaty. How anyone could be sweaty on a cold day such as this, Heidi had no idea. Still, she put that out of her mind and fixed a smile on her face, hoping to win his business.

"Heidi, it's so good to see you. It must be about ..."

"Three or four years," she said as she sat back down.

"Yes, and how's your new venture doing?"

Before she could answer, the waiter appeared and asked what they were drinking.

"What are you having, Heidi?" Frank stared at the drink and turned up his nose. "Is that water?"

"Yes." She knew she'd have to order something alcoholic even if she didn't drink it, otherwise he wouldn't let up. "A gin and tonic for me, thanks."

"And the same for me," he told the waiter. "Now, where were we up to?"

"You asked me how my business was going."

"Yes I did, and how is it doing?"

"It's doing really well. We're breaking records and

rapidly expanding. I'll be looking at opening new offices soon. I'm looking at a new office space in a couple of days."

"Is that so?"

She nodded.

"Have you ever thought about the West Chester area?"

"I'm open to the idea. I've heard there are opportunities there."

He rubbed his nose. "I've got some developments there that I was hoping you might be able to help me out with."

"I'd be happy to."

"But first, I want to talk to you about a forty-story development I've got just one street away from here." He shook his head. "I've got caught up in the housing crunch and they're not selling."

Heidi knew the building he was talking about. "I know, it's been hard lately. There are so many developments and they were all released at the same time. You have to practically give apartments away just to get them sold." She knew him well enough to know the right things to say.

"Exactly, and I'm not going to give them away. That's why I'm inclined to rent them now and put them back on the market at a better time. Who knows? I might just leave them as rentals, if they're doing well that way."

Heidi could barely stop smiling as he continued, giving her specifics and suggested rental amounts. He'd always wanted top dollar for his projects and that was why his properties weren't sold. He was someone who wouldn't be told. Even though developers weren't able to get top dollar for sales, the leasing market was good in comparison. "I think those rents are achievable."

"Do you?"

"Yes."

"And how many people do you have working for you at the moment?"

She told him the number of realtors she had and gave him the 'hard sell.'

"You think you'd be able to lease them fast?" he asked.

"Most of them would be leased inside of two weeks, and some within days. We're continually looking for more apartments to fill the demand. With the rising price of apartments many people have turned to leasing."

He nodded. "I'll email you a list of the apartments and you can liaise with Warren, my assistant. The job's yours." He reached over the table and held out his hand.

She shook it. "Thank you, Frank. I'm excited to get started. We won't let you down."

"I know you won't. I'll call Warren now and let him know what's happening. Are you still in the same building?"

"Yes."

Right after Frank called his assistant, he got an urgent call and had to leave. Since she'd just landed a whole bunch of sought-after apartments to lease, she couldn't wait to get back to the office to get everything prepared and let all her agents know. It was an excellent morale booster to have that news to end the year.

CHAPTER 16

JANELLE WAS the first person she saw when she got back to the office, so naturally she was the first person who heard the news that they had Frank's apartments to lease.

"That's fantastic. I thought you said he never leases any of his projects."

"Times change. There were too many developments on the market in the fall and Frank always charges top dollar for his apartments. So ..."

Janelle said, "Well if you want to sell in this market you have to be realistic."

"And thankfully for us," she said with a grin, "Frank isn't realistic. And good for us, too, that the rental market is still strong. As soon as his assistant sends all the information ... actually, we should have it by now. We'll get them listed on the website asap."

Janelle rubbed her hands together. "I can't wait."

"Me either." Heidi hurried away to find out if Amanda had gotten the information from Warren yet. She hadn't expected to be so busy this close to Christmas. She found Amanda in the boardroom trying to tell the caterers what to do with the decorations.

Heidi sometimes had problems reining Amanda in; she tended to think everything was her job to oversee. She filled Amanda in on what was happening and Amanda scurried off to her office to check her emails.

IT WAS early afternoon and the office party was starting at five. The food always came in at the last minute and the catering staff always handled the decorations and linens, and they supplied all the plates, glasses, and cutlery. *A perfect arrangement,* Heidi thought.

As she leaned against the doorway of the boardroom, Heidi thought back to the Amish gatherings. The simple life was a million miles away. One thing the Amish did well was feed huge crowds of people. It was almost second nature to them. Heidi left the workers to their decorations and headed to find Amanda. She walked into Amanda's cubicle and saw her hunched over her computer with her glasses halfway down her nose. "Anything yet?"

Amanda took her glasses off and looked at her. "Yeah, it's all here. All sixty-two apartments. And he's giving them to us exclusive."

"Wow! Great." Heidi headed to her office feeling pleased with herself for having such good systems in place. If they got all the information and proper documentation that day, they could have them out on the website the next day. "One appointment and it produced so much potential money." She thought back to her first day on the job when no one in the city knew her. It was so hard back then to get a break. Little by little, she made contacts and started making a few sales. Now, with her rentals, she was soaring high in the sky, like an eagle with outstretched wings. A quick look at her computerized sales program brought another smile to her face. They'd leased three apartments between them today going by the green flags on her screen.

A knock on her door caused Heidi to jump. Looking up, she saw her former employee, Macy, in the hallway with her new baby in her arms. Heidi leaped off her chair and hurried to her. "Macy! Show me your baby."

Macy giggled. "Here he is."

When Heidi looked down at the baby, she immediately missed Michael. She stared at the sleeping baby. "Oooh. He's so lovely. What's his name?"

"Andrew."

"That's a beautiful name. Can I hold him?"

Macy giggled again. "Sure you can."

Heidi carefully took him in her arms.

Travis, one of the agents, came up behind Heidi. "Having a baby suits you, Boss." He continued walking with two drinks in his hands.

Heidi laughed. "Hey, the party hasn't started yet."

"It has for me."

She smiled at Macy. "I don't know if babies suit me, but Andrew sure is beautiful. You had better take him back. I might keep him if I have him for too long, at least until he cries." She handed the baby back while Macy laughed. "Are you coming back to work for us?"

"I'm not sure."

"You know, you've always got a job here if you want to come back."

"Thanks. I'll definitely think about it. It depends what happens with Jaden's job."

"Okay. Let me know," Heidi said.

"Thanks. I'll say a quick hello to everyone before I leave."

"Stay for a few drinks. The Christmas party's about to start."

"Thanks, but no, I better get home. I've been out all day."

She watched Macy walk away with Andrew snuggled in her arms. Work had once been everything to Macy, but now her world centered around her baby and her husband. That was something that all the commission checks in the world couldn't buy.

Heidi pushed sentiment aside, and turned her attention to answering emails until she heard loud conversations and music coming from the boardroom. She signed off the last email and headed down the hallway while mentally rehearsing her speech.

Walking into the boardroom, she saw that the catering staff had done a wonderful job, once again. Sparkling gold and white decorations filled the walls and delicate silvery decorations were hung from the ceiling. Plates of delicious finger foods were spread across the table, and in the center of it all was a huge cartoon-like Santa Claus ice sculpture.

Heidi moved around to make sure she spoke to everybody and their significant others. No one was griping about leads today; everyone was finally in the Christmas spirit. When Heidi was between talking to people, she headed over to the food and loaded her plate with several tasty little parcels of pastry filled with meat, and skewered hot vegetable squares.

While she was at the table, she overheard people talking about where they were going to spend Christmas day. She'd been asked quite a few times already where she was spending the day and she'd had her untruthful answer ready. She always used the same made-up story; she was going back to her hometown to see her family and friends.

Everyone knew her story of how she'd come from humble beginnings. No one knew that "humble beginnings" meant she had been a simple Amish girl who once lived on an Amish farm. She didn't mind people knowing she'd been broke, but she didn't want anyone knowing she'd been Amish.

And, she definitely didn't want anyone knowing she was spending Christmas alone. It would be nice to spend Christmas with close friends and family; that wasn't to be. Christmas Day was the hardest day of the year for her. With not being able to do any work, and with no stores open, she generally sat in the apartment by herself and watched movies. It was too hard to go out as it reminded her that everybody was part of a couple or part of a family. That reminded her of Derek Miller, and her parents who had disowned her.

After an hour had passed, she figured she should give her speech and give out the bonuses.

She usually gave her speech at the beginning of the Christmas party while everyone was present but it had gone clean out of her mind. She headed to Brenda who was in charge of the music and asked her to turn it off. Everyone turned to look at her and soon the conversation died down enough for her to speak.

She cleared her throat and hoped she'd memorised her speech well enough. "I just want to thank everyone for being here and for all your hard work during the year. Before I give out the bonuses, I want to say a few words." Her gaze swept over all the staff and their spouses, or boyfriends, or girlfriends, while her assistant got the pile of checks ready. She was dreadful at public speaking and hated talking to more than two people, but she forged ahead regardless. "I want to tell you all that anything is possible. I won't tell you my story again of how I arrived here in this city with nothing, because I'm sure you've all heard it before. I will tell you that I had a dream." She cleared her throat again. Dream was the wrong word to use. It reminded her of Derek and the children. "You see, when you're under pressure, oftentimes that's when you create your best work. Diamonds are created under pressure."

All her staff were smiling and nodding. They loved those sayings she came up with from time to time. Like most salespeople, they were fans of motivational books and seminars. Looking across at them, she thought about the lonely Christmas day that lay ahead. If she'd stayed with Derek and the children until after Christmas, she would've had a day to remember forever.

"Heidi, shall we give out the bonuses now?" her assistant whispered.

Amanda's question made Heidi realize she'd been standing there too long without saying anything.

"Yes, good idea." Heidi decided against giving her prepared speech, and raised her voice. "Who's ready for their Christmas bonuses?"

Everyone cheered. And Heidi looked up and saw Santa Claus walking into the room. It was Travis. He was goofing around as usual.

"Ah, Merry Christmas to all. Christmas bonuses. Let's see. May I?" he put his hands out and Heidi laughed. She nodded to Amanda, who handed him all the envelopes containing the checks.

In his Santa suit, Travis called everyone out in turn and said a little something to each one. It was something that he knew Heidi would have said. He was making fun of her and she didn't mind. It was good to see everyone laughing and having fun.

When most of the people had left, Heidi decided she'd had enough of Christmas cheer.

The caterers would have cleaned up and cleared out by twelve thirty, and Amanda had the job of locking up after them.

"Don't come in until one o'clock tomorrow, Amanda."

"Are you sure?"

"Yes I am. That'll be fine. You earned the extra hours."

"Thanks, Heidi."

Before Heidi left at around eleven, she talked to the remaining few people. Naturally she was asked again where she was spending Christmas day. It seemed that was the main topic of conversation. She gave them the usual answer.

Looking at her watch, she saw it was already eleven, so she headed outside pulling her coat tighter around her glad that another Christmas party was over. The cold wind swept over her, biting into her cheeks. Home wasn't far away, and no taxi would take her that short distance unless she paid extra. Considering taking a taxi regardless, she looked up and down the street but there were none in sight. She'd most likely be home on foot before one drove past.

When she got to her apartment building, she saw the stand-in doorman, the talker, and she just wasn't in the mood, Christmas or not. Once again, she pulled her phone out of her bag and pretended to be talking to someone as she nodded, smiled, and walked past him. When she got into the elevator, she put her phone away.

Pushing open her door, she was engulfed in emptiness and silence. She kicked off her shoes, leaving them at the door, and her coat went the same way—casually dropped on the floor without a care. Then Heidi sat heavily on the couch and put her feet up on the coffee table. Making money was thrilling and exciting, but if she had no one to share it with what was the point of having it?

She pulled Agnes's diary out and dusted it off. Then she sat down on the couch and placed it on the coffee table in front of her.

With a huge sigh, Heidi laid her head back and closed her eyes, wondering what she'd be doing if she was back in her other life with Derek. Right now, she'd give up anything to have his warm arms around her again. Her mind drifted to the children. They would all be in bed by now and so would Derek since he had to get up early in the morning.

When a tear fell down her cheek, she reminded herself of how hard it had been being at home with the children. It wasn't the life for her. She'd already made her choice, twice. Once when she'd left Derek at the bus station, and again when she'd deliberately gone to find Agnes's book at her mother's.

You're being ridiculous, she told herself as she pushed up off the couch and headed to bed. This was her life and she should be pleased with it. Nothing was perfect. Again, she pulled off her clothes and dropped them on the floor not even caring about the mess she was creating.

Normally, she had everything in its place and she hated waking up to an untidy apartment, but tonight she didn't care. She let out a huge sigh as she pulled on her silk nightie that she'd carefully folded and kept neat under the pillow. There was no one to appreciate how tidy and clean she kept the apartment anyway, so it was all a waste of time and effort.

Not wanting to think about Derek and the three children, she deliberately focused her thoughts on several ideas for the new system of distributing leads, drifting into sleep considering how she was going to develop and implement them in the New Year.

CHAPTER 17

Saturday, December 23

HEIDI WOKE REALIZING it was Saturday, the day before Christmas Eve, and she was still in her apartment in New York. No Derek to give her a gentle kiss before he left for work. No girls still asleep. Neither was there a baby to cuddle.

"They're all not real," she reminded herself out loud.

After a few minutes of thinking about them, she forced herself out of bed and jumped into the shower. As the hot water jets pelted her neck and ran down her back she mentally washed away all traces of her Amish life, allowing them to swirl around the drain and disappear. She didn't even want to figure out how she'd gotten back there. Maybe she'd never know except for it having some-thing to do with her grandmother's diary.

While she dried herself with a white fluffy towel, she realized her visualization in the shower hadn't worked. She couldn't get Derek and the children out of her head.

Back in the community, there was a sense of belonging because she was someone's mother, someone's wife, and someone's daughter. There weren't any "mod cons" in the little family home, but neither did she need them. There was a certain sense of contentment in the small house, and she could've gotten used to the slow pace.

Once she was dressed in her usual business suit, she headed out to the living room where she had left Agnes's diary. Picking it up, she hugged it to herself. "Why can't I have a bit of both worlds? Why do I have to choose one or the other?"

She stared down of the diary and thought about Agnes. She was a brave lady to have traveled around the states back in the thirties, or hadn't it been the forties? There were buses back then but there wasn't the transport network that was in place these days. It would've been a lot slower back then too with all the old roads and no freeways. It seemed Agnes's mother had put a great deal of thought into the places to send Agnes, and from her writing, Heidi could tell Agnes had matured with every new place she visited.

Had Agnes been looking for a husband? Heidi wondered. *From her diary notes, it seemed she wasn't interested, but what if she wasn't admitting it to herself?*

Now she was curious where Agnes had met *grossdaddi*. She'd never know, however, because she would never pick up that diary again. It was entirely too risky. There was something about that diary that had given her the apparition and caused her to be in that other life, but thankfully, it had also brought her back.

. . .

SHE SAT down on the couch still perplexed about what had happened to her. *It was God showing me what my life would've been like if I'd stayed,* she told herself. But why was He showing her? It wasn't as though she could change her mind and turn back the clock.

That morning, she'd woken much earlier than normal and had a little time before she had to leave. She changed her mind, and leafed through Agnes's diary to pick up where she'd left off.

Maybe all of it was God's doing, or maybe the answer concerning her visit to the other world could be found within the pages of the diary.

I ARRIVED in Munfordville and it took so long to get here and now I'm really tired. It was arranged that I ride here in a car with Englischers, *a married couple and their teenage daughter, as there are no buses and that was the quickest way to get here. They were all nice and stopped along the way whenever I needed to go to the bathroom, which was quite a few times.*

Elizabeth, Mamm's *cousin, seems really nice. She lives above her store and I'm in one of the two bedrooms.* Mamm *tells me she's never married. I don't know why that is so. All these people tell me that cooking good food is a way to a man's heart and since she's a good cook it doesn't make sense.*

Elizabeth's hair is dark, almost black, with streaks of gray at the front. I think she is about sixty, because I know there are several siblings between them so she's much older than Mamm. *I asked if I could help her in the store tomorrow and she said I could. On the weekend, she will show me how to make jam. I told her I'd* made it before and then she told me that she told my mother she had many secrets to tell me about how to make jams and preserves.

We had a nice talk and then she showed me the bedroom. As I write this I'm nearly falling asleep. More tomorrow.

TODAY WAS my first full day at Elizabeth's house. It seems funny to call her Elizabeth as though she's about my age. Normally I would call her Mrs. something or other or Auntie Elizabeth. She's not my aunt, but somehow she seems like one. Actually, since she's my mother's first-cousin, that makes her my "first-cousin once removed." I'd feel much more comfortable calling her Aunt Elizabeth. I asked her if she wanted me to call her that and she laughed and said no. She said Elizabeth was fine, so I'm getting used to calling someone much older by her first name. Is that her way of saying she's viewing me as an adult instead of a child?

Elizabeth's normal routine is to eat breakfast and then open her store, even if it's before eight o'clock. Today we opened the doors right at eight o'clock, after our breakfast of scrambled eggs and Elizabeth's freshly-made doughnuts. First she showed me how to hang up the shingle and place the A-frame sign close to the road, advertising the jams and pickles that she sells.

The bottom floor of the house is taken up with the store, and there is a little kitchen out the back. When there are no customers she's back there cooking, and she leaves off the cooking when the bell of the front door rings. Today I was able to sell things for her, and she kept cooking. That seemed to make her happy. She told me she's usually there by herself with no help.

She didn't make a lot of money today, but she says that it's just enough for her to live on. That explains why she doesn't hire help.

I made the suggestion that she knock out the wall between the store and the kitchen because people might like to watch her cook and see how the jams and preserves are made.

She told me people wouldn't want to see that and also the kitchen got too messy. I didn't argue with her, but I thought she might get more customers if she made the store more interesting. That's what I'd do if I owned the store.

For the evening meal, we went two houses down the road to Eunice's house. It seems Eunice and Elizabeth are best friends. I am here for nearly another week, and if this place is anything like the other places, Malachi Arnold will soon appear. I don't know where he will stay.

I'm starting to think that my mother's secret plan was Malachi Arnold, like I wrote before. I'm guessing that she wants me to marry him, and that's why he appears everywhere. I wonder if he knows what is going on or whether my mother has given him some other reasons to be at all these different places. She can be quite bossy when she wants to be, and many people look on my parents as parental figures and that's probably because of Dat being a deacon. Anyway, I will soon find out. That's all for tonight, my eyes are fast closing, and I need some sleep.

P. S. I know my sly-as-a-fox Mamm has something to do with Malachi's travels, just as she arranged mine.

IT's the next night now — Friday. Malachi Arnold has not appeared, so I'm beginning to think I might've been wrong. Perhaps the long journey to Munfordville put him off coming here. The good thing about being here is that Elizabeth is teaching me a lot about the art of jam making. And that life can be happy as an unmarried Amish woman.

· · ·

Now it is Sunday; I didn't write yesterday because nothing else happened and Saturday was the same as Friday. I've been to the very small meeting today, and was surprised to see that there were only three families plus a couple of single men. The single men kept their distance. I wonder if they think I'm there to find a husband. There was one surprise for me at the meeting, and that was Malachi Arnold showed after all. I was shocked to see him. He's staying at the bishop's house. When I asked him why he was there, he looked down at his feet and mumbled something about traveling around. He gave the same story as before.

Now I know for certain he's following me. He must be in love with me. He's a nice man, but I'm waiting to see if more develops. Surely there should be something extra in a man. If I was choosing with my head like I intended to, I would think Malachi Arnold would be a good choice especially since my parents like him. Now I'm not so sure if that's the best way to pick a husband. Anyway, I'm not in a hurry even if my parents are.

It was no surprise to me that Elizabeth invited Malachi for dinner tomorrow night. I'll try to find out then what is going on and what my parents told him.

When we came home from the meeting earlier, Elizabeth told me that she loves to sew, but by the time she's put in a full day at work she's too tired. I told her that once she shows me how to do everything, I will run the store for her until I leave and she can sew as much as she wants. That made her really happy. Although, I could tell she was hesitant in leaving me to do everything. I told her I'm a fast learner and I can do it all. I hope she allows me to do it because she is such a nice lady and I would like to do something for her before I leave. Also, it would be good for me to know how to make everything and how to serve the customers that come in.

Because I feel so comfortable with Elizabeth, I told her about

Malachi Arnold and how he appears everywhere I've been. She agrees with me that it sounds like a plan of Mamm's. *She had a real laugh about it.*

Now, as I'm writing this, I think Mamm *must've told her the plan too because she did ask Malachi to come to dinner. I know for a certainty that* Mamm *told everybody at the previous places I stayed of her plan to have me marry Malachi. It wasn't that much of a secret, if that's what* Mamm *was talking to* Dat *about that night when I overheard them talking about me. A 'secret plan' she called it. She should've called it an 'obvious plot' rather than a secret plan. Not really a plot either, she should've called it … I don't really know. I don't like anyone interfering in my life, not even* Mamm. Dat *would've kept out of it. I'm sure he didn't have anything to do with it.*

Anyway, I told Elizabeth I would make the evening meal for Malachi if she didn't mind. She said I could. For dessert, I'm making the doughnuts that I learned to make at Aunt Elsie's. I don't know what I'll make for the rest of it. It depends what I can buy at the markets. I'm looking forward to having the kitchen to myself. Elizabeth said that weekdays early in the week aren't busy, so I can have the kitchen all to myself from mid-afternoon. I hope I can talk to Malachi alone and find out the truth of why he's here. I'm sure he didn't buy any horses either, from Aunt Sally and Onkel *Abel.*

I'm writing the recipe for doughnuts below so I never forget it. We never have them at home. I'll cook them all the time when I get back.

Doughnuts: (Makes around fifteen)
Ingredients:

Half a pound of flour
2 teaspoons of baking powder
One pinch of salt
One pinch of nutmeg
4 tablespoons of butter
¼ cup of sugar
Two eggs
Half a cup of milk
Caster sugar (also called superfine sugar)
One lemon

Method:
Sift together: flour, baking powder, salt, and nutmeg.
Rub in butter, add sugar, then well beaten eggs, and sufficient milk to mix into a soft dough.
Turn onto a floured board
Roll out a cord half an inch thick
Cut into rings with the doughnut cutter.
Fry until doughnuts are golden brown.
Sprinkle with caster sugar and serve hot with slices of lemon.

I'VE ONLY JUST FINISHED CLEANING up after dinner and Elizabeth and I have gone to bed without our usual evening tea and chatting because it's so late. Malachi came to dinner and, just as he walked in the door, other visitors arrived. We ended up with three extra people for dinner and I was so pleased I'd made enough. Aunt Elsie told me to always make extra. The visitors were Wilma and her husband, Joseph, and Wilma's sister, Florence. It was a surprise visit as Wilma lived a distance away and she and Elizabeth normally wrote to one another.

Tonight, everyone enjoyed the roast I made, or said they did. I was pleased too tonight because Florence gave me her recipe for sauerbraten and spaetzle. It's a lot of trouble to make, but it's worth it. Spaetzle is like dumplings, but they are really noodles. They go so well with the Sauebraten.

Sauerbraten (for this recipe the beef needs to be marinated for two days)
Ingredients:
2 lbs beef
Marinade:
Ingredients:
1/2 cup water
1/2 cup red wine
1/2 cup vinegar
2 tbsp mustard seeds
2 small onions
5 cloves
2 bay leaves
2 cups of mixed celery, stems and leaves
1 tbsp parsley root, cut
1 leek
salt and pepper to taste
Method:
Mix the red wine, water, vinegar, cloves, mustard seeds, and bay leaves.
Bring it to a boil and let it simmer for 10 minutes.

When it cools add the vegetables.
Rub the marinade all over the beef and seal the dish and leave in your refrigerator for two days, turning over at least a few times a day.

After two days: Remove beef from marinade, drain marinade through a sieve. Keep the marinade liquid (discard the vegetables).

Rinse the meat and pat dry.
Heat butter and brown the beef briskly on high temperature.
Add some marinade, reduce temperature.
Cover with a lid and let it cook for ninety min, pouring small amounts of marinade over the beef frequently until the marinade is used up.
Remove beef from pan, wrap it in a tea towel to keep warm. (modern equivalent aluminium foil).
Mix cornstarch with cold water, add it to the broth while stirring continuously
Spice with salt and, pepper, and then add a pinch of sugar.

Spaetzle (serves six)
Ingredients:
1 cup plain flour
1/4 cup milk
2 eggs
1/2 teaspoon ground nutmeg
1 pinch freshly ground white pepper
1/2 teaspoon salt
8 ½ pints hot water (just more than a gallon)

2 tablespoons butter

2 tablespoons chopped fresh parsley

Method:

Mix together flour, salt, white pepper and nutmeg. Beat eggs well, and add alternately with the milk to the dry ingredients. Mix until smooth.

Press dough through a large- holed sieve.

Drop a few at a time into simmering liquid.

Cook 5 to 8 minutes.

Drain well.

Lightly fry cooked spaetzle in butter.

Sprinkle fresh parsley over spaetzle before serving.

IT WAS hard to get a chance to talk to Malachi and ask if my mother had suggested he follow me from place to place. He told everyone at the table he was visiting the countryside and that my mother and father had suggested different communities where they knew people. I still didn't have my answer, because it could've been a coincidence. I might have made a fool out of myself if I'd said anything to him.

Then Malachi said something that surprised me; he's leaving tomorrow and going somewhere else. I couldn't find out where because too many people were talking at once. I was a little upset that I wouldn't see more of him. I've known him so long, yet I don't really know him properly. I know he's a good person and he's nice and polite. I don't even know what he thinks of me. I guess he thinks I'm okay. Okay as a friend, but does he think I could be more than that? In a couple of days, I leave for Oakland, Mary-

land. That's another long, long journey. I'm glad I'm not traveling in the winter. The days have been mild. I'll be staying with the bishop and his wife.

From there I'm going to Morgantown, West Virginia, which is not far from Oakland. Then I'm going to York, which is right close to home. I'm at the halfway point of my trip now and have learned many things.

Things I have learnt so far; I've learned a lot about cooking, how to make bread and pies, and how to run a household. I have also learned that I'm not lazy as all my family kept telling me. And I'm learning to view myself as an adult. Also ... I think I might like Malachi. At least I'm curious now. Mamm and Dat *had many people over to the house because of* Dat *being a deacon and Malachi is just another one of those people who spend time at the house in fellowship.*

I never liked anybody before in that way, but now I'm starting to think about him all the time. Is that love? Or the beginnings of it?

Amy and Harold liked each other from the time they were young teenagers. Everybody always knew that they would get married and now they're getting married soon. I'll be the last child of my family to remain unmarried. That's okay, though, because I am the youngest and that is to be expected.

If whoever is reading this doesn't know about the history of my family, Amy and Harold would have got married earlier, but Harold left with his brother to build a community up north. Amy asked him not to go, but Harold went anyway. They wrote to each other and one year later Harold came back. It took another year for Amy to agree to marry him. I asked why she didn't marry him quickly, and she never gave me a proper answer. I know she was upset that he went away when she didn't want him to, and I think she was deliberately making him wait longer because of that, maybe to be sure he wouldn't go off again.

Love is complicated. I don't know why Harold went away if he was in love with Amy. Why didn't he marry Amy first, and take her with him? It would've saved me having to talk to her every night until very late to stop her from crying. I had to keep saying, 'of course he'll come back to you. Nee, he won't meet someone else. He loves you, he'll be back.'

I could only hope my words were true, and I think I was more pleased than anyone when Harold came back and asked Amy to marry him.

HEIDI CLOSED THE BOOK. Even going back generations, love was complicated. She agreed with Amy. If Harold had loved her why did he leave? Probably for the same reasons Heidi got on that bus and left Derek. In his youth, Harold might have thought nothing of love, the way Heidi had disregarded her love for Derek and Derek's love for her.

CHAPTER 18

WHEN HEIDI CLOSED Agnes's diary and looked at the time, she remembered she hadn't fixed her face yet, and she headed back to the bathroom. Once she had applied her usual makeup, she gathered her things and headed off to her favorite café for breakfast.

That morning, everything reminded her of Derek and the children. Everywhere she looked, she saw babies and loving couples and cute little girls.

JUST AFTER EIGHT, she arrived at work and headed to her office. She was the first one there. The next to arrive would be the two receptionists who arrived at eight thirty. She remembered that her assistant, Amanda, wouldn't be in until one.

Hardly any appointments were booked for that day and half the agents wouldn't even come into the office. The business would be closed between the twenty fourth and the twenty sixth, and then there would be a skeleton staff until after the New Year. People just weren't interested in looking at apartments over the Christmas-to-New Year's Day period, but history told her they would start again in earnest on the second of January.

This close to Christmas, there were fewer emails to reply to and everything had already wound down. It was hardly worth the effort to go to work. That was to be expected at this time of year, but she didn't like the lack of work because that also meant more time to fill and more time to feel lonely.

She grabbed a blank notepad from the filing cabinet and, taking pen in hand, she jotted down some ideas to take her business to the next level. On top of the list was getting her staff and the leads-distribution situation sorted. For the next ten minutes, she mulled over a few ideas she thought might work. She needed Janelle's input, since she was one of the main agents in the company.

As some of the staff began to arrive, dragging their feet as though forced to be here, she realized none of them were as hungry to get ahead as she'd been when she had started. The difference was most likely that she had no family to return to if things suddenly went bad. She had no backstop. Her parents attitude had hurt her deeply, especially when she knew other Amish parents allowed their children who'd left the Amish to visit, so why couldn't her parents? If they were trying to make her come back by disowning her, it hadn't worked.

Heidi turned to her computer and did an Internet search to see if her father had died. She'd been too nervous to do it before, but she had to know. The first thing that popped up was a small article in a Lancaster newspaper. He was dead. He was one of fifteen Amish people who'd died around five years ago from a flu epidemic in one of the coldest winters on record. She covered her mouth with her hand as tears threatened. It was true, her father was dead and no one had thought to find her and tell her. She wouldn't have been hard to find since she hadn't even changed her name and they'd known she was headed for New York.

An email popped up on her screen; Amanda, who frequently worked from home before and after hours. The accountant had called and had postponed his appointment with her today, rebooking it in early January. Besides that, Frank, the developer, wanted an urgent meeting with her. *Uh-oh. That doesn't sound good.*

Immediately, Heidi called Frank and got Warren, his assistant, and made an appointment to meet his boss. Frank was booked all day, despite his insistence of urgency, and she'd have to wait until five o'clock to find out why he wanted to see her.

Next on the list was a meeting out of the office with Janelle.

Janelle answered the phone by saying, "I'm only five minutes away."

"I'm not calling about that. I was wondering if you want to go to lunch today?"

"Again?"

Heidi leaned back in her chair. "Are you complaining?"

"No. That would work. I've only got two appointments today. One at ten and one at three."

"Good because I've got something I want to discuss with you."

"You're not letting me go, are you?"

Heidi chuckled and picked up her list of ideas she'd jotted down. "Of course not. I've got some ideas for next year that I'd like your input on."

"Sure. There's something I've been meaning to tell you, too."

"What is it?"

"I'll tell you over lunch."

"Okay." Heidi hoped Janelle wasn't going to say she was leaving. "Meet me in my office at twelve and we'll go from there." She ended the call to Janelle and then called Amanda. "I'm having lunch today with Janelle. Could you book us a table for two and make it somewhere nice, but not too far away?"

"Sure. What time?"

"Make it for twelve thirty. And can you add the appointment I made with Frank for five o'clock tonight?"

"Okay. Did he say what it was about?"

"Beats me. I only spoke to his assistant."

"Okay. I'm here."

Heidi looked up to see that Amanda was standing in her office doorway with a bag over her shoulder and a take-out coffee in her hand. Heidi laughed and put her phone down. "I didn't even see you there. I told you not to show up until one."

Amanda handed Heidi the take-out coffee. "Here."

"Thanks."

"I figured out that you didn't see me, and I got bored at home so I figured I might as well work here where everything I need is at my fingertips."

"How long have you been standing there?"

Amanda giggled. "Only since I asked you what time to book the restaurant."

Heidi gave a little laugh. "Text me, please, and let me know where you decide to book us for lunch. Nowhere too expensive."

"Got it. Is that all?"

"Yes, thanks."

With a quick smile, Amanda headed to her office, which was really a small cubicle off from the large open-plan office the realtors occupied.

It'd be disappointing if Frank took his apartments from them, and until Heidi found out what he wanted, she knew she'd be concerned. She didn't want to be negative, but the only reason she could think of for this sudden and unexpected appointment was that he'd changed his mind. Maybe some other agency had stuck their nose in and said something to cause him to change his mind about leasing his apartments. Or...could it have been another company trying to get in good with Frank and steal his business away from her?

Work always came with worries. Sometimes it was a constant juggling act. She took a deep breath and, exhaling slowly, she let the worry slide off her. If Frank was trying to get out of their agreement, she'd deal with that when she heard it from his own lips. Otherwise, there was no use worrying. She turned her attention back to her plans and worked on them until lunchtime.

· · ·

"Is this a drinking lunch?" Janelle asked when she got to the restaurant and sat down at the table with Heidi.

"No, not if you've got another appointment this afternoon. I've got one and I know you've got one too." Heidi jiggled her straw in the ice in her drink. "I was thirsty, so I couldn't wait. It's only tomato juice."

"Well, it's about time I gave up drinking anyway."

She stared at Janelle. It was an odd thing for her to say since she was never one to say no to a drink. "Is that so? You're not sick or anything, are you?"

"No."

"Then why—"

"I'm pregnant."

She stared at her friend's red lips as they curved into a smile. "No!"

"I am. It's something that just happened; we weren't even planning for it, not yet."

Heidi's fingertips flew to her lips and her stomach churned with a mixture of emotions. Life was passing her by. She was close to thirty and had no family and not even a boyfriend. Motherhood was only something she'd experienced in her vision. Then her thoughts turned to Michael and how sweet he was. Where was he? Did he need her? All she could do was hold her stomach.

"Well, aren't you pleased for me?"

"Yes, you just caught me by surprise. Congratulations. That's really wonderful news." Heidi leaned over and kissed her friend on her cheek.

"When we have good news, we normally have bubbly. We can't do that today," Janelle said.

"Correction, you normally have bubbly. I rarely drink, and I don't care for champagne."

"That's true." Janelle laughed.

Then Heidi realized her fears were coming to fruition. "You're leaving?"

"I still want to work for as long as I can."

That was good news for Heidi. "And what about after the baby's born?"

"Scott is going to start working from home, so he'll go part time and look after the baby. We'll hire a part-time nanny to help out. It's a perfect arrangement."

Heidi was pleased. "It certainly sounds like it. So, you'll only have a few weeks off?"

"That's right, the usual six weeks."

The waiter came up to take their orders and after they had made their selections, Janelle asked Heidi, "What did you want to see me about?"

"I touched on it briefly with you before. I've got a couple of ideas for next year and I want to run them by you." Heidi pulled some papers from her handbag and proceeded to go over the ideas for the new-lead distribution guidelines. Janelle was agreeable when she heard she was going to be overseeing a certain number of agents. She'd be responsible for training and then receive remuneration from their sales.

"I like it. I think the receptionists had too much power over who got the leads. I'm not complaining, mind you, but I can see why the others were."

Heidi stared at Janelle. "I can't believe you're going to be a mother."

"Neither can I."

"When did you find out exactly?"

"We've known for a couple of weeks. We figured it was too early to tell anyone. I still haven't told anyone, only you because you're my boss. We're keeping it quiet for another couple of months."

"I understand. My lips are sealed."

Janelle laughed.

A small part of Heidi couldn't help being envious of her good friend. She had a good husband and now she was going to become a mother. Why hadn't it happened for her?

"We'll have to find you a good man. Are you sure you don't want to meet—"

"No, don't ask me again." Heidi raised her hands wondering if her friend was a mind reader. "The thing is, I can't stop thinking about someone I knew a long time ago. We were dating when I left … when I left home to come here."

Janelle's eyes opened wide. "Have you been in touch with him lately?"

Heidi shook her head.

"Why not?"

"I don't know." Heidi squirmed in her chair, already sorry she'd said anything.

"Have you looked him up on Facebook, or anything?"

"He's a very private person. He wouldn't be on any social media or anything like that."

"Are you sure? Maybe he's changed from how he was so many years ago. People do change, you know."

Heidi shrugged her shoulders again and told a little white lie. "I've looked and he's not on anything." She could hold it in no longer. Heidi had to tell someone about her vision, dream, or whatever it had been. "The other night, I had this amazing lifelike dream that I was married to him and had three children. It was so lifelike it was eerie." She didn't tell Janelle that she'd had no idea who "Heidi King" was when Heidi called her, or that just as many days had passed here as had passed in her dream.

"Don't you see, Heidi?"

"What?"

"It's a sign that you have to find him. Look him up when you go home."

"I don't know about that. Someone like him would've been snapped up pretty quick. He would already be married." She looked down into her tomato juice. "Small-town guys like him always marry small-town girls, and they marry young."

The waiter brought their drinks to them. Janelle had sparkling water, while Heidi had ordered a second tomato juice.

When the waiter left, Janelle said, "Ah, yes, I know the kind of town you're talking about. That's why I like the city. Anyway, you must've had that dream for a reason. Maybe it was a sign you should try dating again."

"I can't. I've had too many disappointments."

"Dating is just like sales. It's a numbers game. If you keep swinging that bat you're bound to hit a home run sooner or later."

"I don't know."

Janelle grabbed her iPhone. "What's his name? I'm looking him up to see what I can find out about him."

"No. Forget him. I'm not going to tell you his name."

"Aw, come on."

Heidi shook her head. "No. Not telling."

"I think you're in love with this guy."

"I was a long time ago and I didn't value what I had. I thought love was something easy to find, if you know what I mean. I thought I'd find it again."

"Love isn't easy to come by. I can tell you that. I can't tell you how many people I had to date before I found Scott."

"And you're lucky, he's perfect for you."

"I wouldn't have found him if I hadn't dated a lot of people."

Heidi smiled at her friend, who was still trying to make her point and still hoping she'd go on a blind date with that retired baseball player. Heidi shook her head once more. "Not going to happen."

"What?"

"I'm not going to date your husband's friend."

"Suit yourself. I'm just trying to help."

"I know, and thank you."

"How often do you think about this Mr. X of yours? What was his name again?"

"Nice try, but I'm still not going to tell you. I just think about him every now and again. I guess every few months, and well … around the holidays. I've been thinking of him nearly every day lately and then I had that weird lifelike dream. It went on over a few days. I've never had a dream like it, so real. It was really weird."

"If I were you I would go back home over Christmas. Oh wait, you said you *are* going back home at Christmas."

Heidi frowned at Janelle, wondering if Janelle knew

she was lying about going back home. "I've never bumped into him when I've been back." She felt bad telling her friend lies about where she was going to spend Christmas, but it was better than Janelle knowing the truth.

"This time, try to find him. Find out where he works, and show up there."

Heidi giggled. "I couldn't do that."

"Well, could you please at least find out if he's married or not?"

"I suppose I could do that."

"Good. I feel as if I'm getting somewhere now. I've got a good feeling about this guy. I haven't seen you like this before about anyone."

"Like what?"

"All nervous and acting weirdly. And you've been dreaming about him. That's always a good sign."

"Maybe. Now let's talk about you. I just can't believe you're having a baby."

"Me either."

When Janelle started talking about her plans for the baby, Heidi tried to act like she was listening intently, when instead she was thinking about Derek and the children. She had a family in another dimension, and she regretted returning to this one so quickly. One bad day and she was ready to check out? She'd never been one to give up on something so easily.

It made sense that even in a perfect world there would be good days and bad days, not every day in someone's life would be perfect even if they had the best luck in the world. It was only normal for the children to test their boundaries. What child wouldn't want to run in the rain and play in the snow, even roll in the snow? Heidi remembered doing that herself when she was young, yet when her own children did it, she couldn't handle it. It'd been daunting to be unexpectedly thrust into motherhood instead of easing her way into it. One day she was single, and the next she had three children and a husband.

When Janelle drew a breath, Heidi said, "Dessert?"

"We haven't eaten yet."

"Oh. Rats! Dessert sounds perfect."

Janelle laughed, and at that moment the waiter placed their food in front of them.

Heidi thanked him and stared at her chicken salad, which was tiny. It was nothing like the portions of Amish food. That was something else she missed—hearty food and lots of it. "I meant after this, would you want dessert?"

"Of course, I'm eating for two now. I'm definitely going to need dessert."

"Good. Then I'll have to have a dessert as well to keep you company."

Both women giggled.

CHAPTER 19

AT FIVE O'CLOCK, Heidi was waiting for Frank Dyson at the same table at the same bar where they'd met the previous day. He walked in grinning from ear-to-ear, and from the look on his face it didn't seem like he was going to renege on their deal.

"Heidi, how are you?"

She stood up to greet him, and as usual, he kissed her on both cheeks. She noticed he was clean-shaven this afternoon, not sweaty, and more presentably dressed.

When they sat down, he ordered a drink. "Do you want something to eat? Another drink?"

"No, but thanks. I'll just stick with my sparkling water with lime." This time, she wasn't concerned about what he thought about her not drinking. "What is it you wanted to see me about?"

"I had no idea this morning, and that's what I wanted to see you about."

She thought back over what he said. It didn't make sense. "I'm sorry. No idea about what?"

"I thought you and I could go to dinner tonight and then head to Las Vegas for Christmas."

She was so shocked she burst out laughing. Then her laughter subsided when she realized he was making an indecent proposal. "Frank, you're married, aren't you?"

"Yes, but my wife's away for Christmas. I had no idea she was going away until this morning."

Heidi couldn't believe what she heard. She ran a hand over her head, raking through her cropped hair. It was such an awkward situation. "No. I'm sorry, I just can't do that."

He leaned forward. "I've always liked you, Heidi." He reached out and touched her hand, and she pulled it away.

"This relationship has to be purely business, Frank. I respect you as a developer and a businessman, and as a professional friend, but anything else is totally out of the question."

He straightened up and his jaw stiffened. Gone was his smile and she was sure she was going to lose the business he'd just given her. "I'm putting a lot of business your way."

"And I appreciate it, and in return, my staff and I are going to make you a lot of money."

He stared at her for a while, chuckled, and then wagged his finger at her. "I'm not going to give up on you."

"When it comes to this, you should. This relationship is just business and that's all it'll ever be. I've got no idea what made you think otherwise." She gave a little tremble.

"Do you have a boyfriend?" he asked with rising eyebrows.

Derek popped into her mind. "Yes, I'm practically married."

The waiter brought him his drink.

When the waiter left, he said, "Tell me more about this man you're practically married to."

"No, I don't talk about him. With you and me." She pointed to him and then pointed to herself. "This relationship we have is not going to go where you want it to—ever, so if you expect anything more or if I gave you the wrong impression somehow, I'm sorry. If that means you'll take your business away then do it."

He breathed out heavily. "A deal is a deal, and we shook on it. I just thought we could have a nice time in Las Vegas."

"I'm glad we understand each other. Now, I need to know you'll never say anything like that to me again." She folded her arms and stared at him.

He smiled. "I won't. You shouldn't be so beautiful, though. I mean, what's a man to do?"

While she sipped on her drink, she wondered why life was often such a battle. "As soon as I finish this drink, I have to go. I need to get your apartments leased."

"That's what I like to hear."

AFTER A LONG DRAWN OUT DAY, and with the stressful meeting at the end of it, Heidi opened the door of her apartment and kicked off her shoes. What if the reason she'd never found love in New York City was because she'd been meant to marry Derek?

Before she heated her dinner, she settled down to read some more of her grandmother's diary.

Today I arrived in Oakland Maryland. I can only write a little bit because it's so late and I need to get some sleep.

I've been here a day now, staying with Bishop Silas and his wife, Leah. I found out my mother writes to Leah a lot and they take part in circle letters. They're the letters that keep arriving at the house. The bishop's house was full of people all day. Leah explained that they have twelve kinner *and the younger ones in the* haus *are her* grosskinner. *Since the older three are married and have twelve* kinner *between them, Leah looks after the young ones during the day. I don't think I've ever met a happier woman than Leah. No matter what I say she laughs about it. She's a happy person to be around.*

When there was a quiet moment, I asked, "When is Malachi Arnold arriving?"

She put her hand over her mouth and giggled loudly. "That's supposed to be a surprise," she said. "Malachi will be here the day after tomorrow," she finally told me.

I told her he has appeared everywhere I've stayed, and she pressed her lips together and didn't say any more.

Bishop Silas is a quiet man and at first I thought that was because he didn't like me, or didn't want me there. I've watched him today, though, and saw he's like that with everyone. The house here is very small and I don't know where everybody sleeps. They put me in the attic, which is small and only has room for one bed and one nightstand. I have my bag in front of the nightstand and there's no place for anything else. I can't hang any of my dresses because I'm under the part of the roof where it slants. It's hot there, but not too hot to prevent me sleeping.

One of Leah's grosskinner, a cute little boy of around six, told me that I'm staying in his playroom. I said I was very sorry and I wouldn't be staying there for long–just a few days. He got into trouble for saying that to me and this time Leah wasn't laughing. Her words were stern and she frowned. I felt a little bad for him and when I saw him sitting alone, I wanted to suggest that I play with him. I wanted to make it up with him, but Leah had me too busy in the kitchen.

Today I'm starting to miss home. It sounded like a big adventure when I started and I'm glad I have traveled long distances, but I'm always tired afterward. I miss Furball. I miss him sleeping on my bed and seeing him during the day under the covers as a lump on my bed. He's just always there, ready for me to stroke his gray fur. When I speak to him softly, he stretches out and paws at the air and purrs loudly. I like cats because they don't demand anything and are just there when you want to talk to them. They don't come chasing after you like dogs do. At least, Furball doesn't.

TODAY, Leah's oldest daughter, Becky, who isn't married, collected me and took me back to her house. She showed me what she does for a living. She makes clay tiles and I can't believe she sells enough of them to make enough money to live on. The tiles are really pretty. She takes them to the markets to sell them, and sometimes she sells them at roadside stalls.

I asked Becky what kind of clay she uses and she said she uses the kind of clay that teacups are made out of. She does it all out in her barn and she has three big kilns. There were so many different *patterns of tiles. I can't imagine someone tiling a whole kitchen with these tiles but perhaps they'd look good with a few in amongst a whole lot of plain tiles. That might look all right. She showed me how the tiles are fired in a kiln, pressed, then glazed. Once they're glazed it gives them a lovely smooth surface to apply the decorations. They even used pictures from postcards on some of the tiles, by tracing the pictures by hand, and then lastly putting them in the kiln again.*

I was at Becky's place for a good part of the day and she even let me make a tile. I traced one of the pictures and then it was put into the kiln. Then she took me back to Leah's in time to help with the evening meal. It was such a wonderful day and she said she'd bring the tile over when it was finished firing and I could take it home with me.

Tomorrow is the Sunday meeting and it's to be held at Becky's house. She said there were going to be three baptisms.

READING about the meeting and baptism reminded Heidi that she couldn't see herself living in the community, in the closed off life and wearing those shapeless clothes. She was an individual, and the idea of the community was to play down individuality. But didn't God see everybody as individuals? *If the very hairs on our head are numbered, surely we are individuals in God's sight?*

The trouble was, she thought differently than everybody else in the community. Heidi wasn't about to just take what the oversight leaders told her. She questioned things and there were things that couldn't be explained, like what had happened to her.

With a better understanding of who her grandmother

was, she threw the book down on the coffee table and then headed to put her dinner in the microwave. It was the same old routine, but tonight, she didn't even bother surfing through the TV channels. She grabbed her dinner out of the microwave, sat on her wide window seat and looked down at the traffic and the crowds. As she ate, she watched the world go by.

LATER THAT EVENING, emptiness washed over Heidi. She yearned for her comfortable Amish home, her *kinner*, and Derek. She'd give up everything just for another moment with them. That was where she belonged. She knew that now, but had she left things too late? Had she sacrificed her opportunity when she asked God to bring her back to New York City?

Emptiness gnawed at her heart.

CHAPTER 20

THAT NIGHT, she picked up her grandmother's diary again and prayed to go back home, back to Derek and the children. In the brief time she'd been with them, she'd found looking after the children tough, but at times it had been wonderful. All of life had ups and downs and she wanted to spend them all with her family—the good times and the bad.

She turned her face up to heaven and prayed once more. "God, if any of this is real and I can go to my other reality, I'm asking you to please take me back to Derek and my family. I feel that is where I belong. Amen." To help her prayers be answered, she took her grandmother's book to bed, so she could replicate exactly what she had done when she'd crossed dimensions the last two times.

SHE OPENED the book at the last entry anxious to know if Agnes had married the man she was falling for. Had

SAMANTHA PRICE

Agnes's mother arranged for Malachi to be everywhere Agnes went?

These were the last pages of her grandmother's entries. If God blessed Heidi and by some miracle she ended back with the children and Derek, she'd try every last one of the recipes Agnes had recorded.

She could barely stay awake, but she found she couldn't wait to find out which of those men had become her grandfather. Even though she'd never met her paternal grandmother, now she knew her. Perhaps that's why Agnes had kept a diary, for the following generations to learn from.

I'M STARTING to see a pattern as I go from place to place. Everybody seems to be an expert on one special thing, or some special dish. I wonder what Leah's speciality is. Dinner tonight was nice, but it was just plain old roasted chicken and roasted vegetables. That was that. It was nice, but there was no special recipe and no secrets to learn. All there was to do was put the meat and the vegetables in the oven. Anybody could do that.

What speciality does Leah have? She must have one and I'm going to ask her tomorrow.

HEIDI TURNED the page to keep reading. "Ah, this must be the next night because she starts on a new page," she said to herself.

• • •

I FOUND out that Leah is an expert bread maker. I thought that's what Aunt Elsie was, but Aunt Elsie could do everything well. Leah told me that one of the things about making bread was to knead the dough very well to make sure there are no air bubbles.

Before I started making bread, I thought that the more air in the dough, the more it would rise, but no, that's not right. I mentioned that to Leah, and she laughed.

Leah also said to let it stand for a good forty minutes before putting it into the oven and the dough should double in size. To check if it's ready, put your thumb into the dough about an inch, if the mixture springs back into place, it's not ready to go into the oven. If the hole stays there, it's ready to be baked.

It also shocked me to learn that the weather can affect the bread. No one had ever told me that before.

Once the bread is done, Leah said to take it out of the pan immediately so it doesn't sweat.

Leah has a special bread starter that was her mother's and she will give some of it to me to take when I leave. She said if I use the bread starter and follow her instructions exactly, then my bread should be every bit as good as hers. If it isn't, she said to keep trying and keep at it.

Because there are so many mouths to feed at the house here, Leah makes bread every day. The smell of the bread reminds me so much of home.

I'm excited because Malachi is arriving tomorrow. He'll be staying at Leah's oldest son's house. I met him today, his name is James and his wife is Emily. Their son, Caleb, is the one who's annoyed because I'm sleeping in the attic space that he says is his playroom. That's all I can write now because I'm so tired. I'm more than half way through the pages in this book. I hope the pages *don't run out before I get back home. There are no mercantiles around here to buy another one just like this one.*

DAY three of staying with Leah and the bishop. Malachi arrived today. I was having a break from the kitchen duties and was out in the yard playing catch with Caleb when a buggy drove up to the house. I held my breath and hoped it was Malachi, and it was. James had brought Malachi to say hello to his (James's) parents.

I had a chance to talk to him when Caleb ran to his father. Malachi gave me a big smile and I asked him what he was doing there.

He said again that he was just traveling around. I asked him if he thought it strange that we keep seeing each other and he said he didn't think it was. Now I know that he is without a clue that my mother is trying to pair us together. If he knew, we could've laughed about it. Before I could say anything, Leah came out of the house to greet him. She invited him to dinner that night and James asked if they could come tomorrow instead because his wife had already cooked a special dinner for tonight. So now I get to see Malachi tomorrow night for dinner here at the house.

I'm looking forward to making more bread tomorrow. I didn't know it was so involved. There definitely is a difference in the taste and texture between Leah's bread and Mamm's. I guess that means it's worth the extra effort.

Before he left, James asked me if I would like to go with Malachi tomorrow and have a look at James's onkel's place where he makes buggies. I looked over at Leah to see if she would mind. I didn't know if my mother would like me doing something without the approval of my host family.

Leah smiled and suggested that I go along and said I'd enjoy it. Now I'm seeing a lot of Malachi tomorrow.

James is coming to the house at ten to get me and then bringing me back in the mid-afternoon. I guess that will be in time to help Leah with the dinner. Anyway, if I'm late, there are plenty of other helpers here. Her two teenage girls are fourteen and fifteen. They are nothing like Leah. They are quiet and more like their father. The rest of Leah and the bishop's kinner are boys.

Now it's day four at Leah's and I've already been to the buggy-maker's. Today has been the best day of my life. I got such a surprise when I was waiting outside for James and then when the buggy pulled up I saw that the driver of the buggy was Malachi. It turns out that James couldn't come at the last minute, and Malachi had been given directions to the place with the buggies. I wasn't really interested in seeing how they made buggies. I've seen enough of it before, back in my community. I only said yes to James so I could spend more time with Malachi.

If I'd known it was just going to be Malachi and me, I might have talked to Leah and organized a picnic basket. I could tell by the look on Malachi's face he was pleased to be taking me to the Wilsons' buggy making yard.

MR. WILSON WAS WAITING outside when we got there. He was wearing a straw hat, and he had a long white beard and thin-rimmed round glasses, and he was wearing dark gray pants and a long-sleeved lighter-gray shirt.

He told us that Amish buggies were always changing. The wheels were changing and he was now making wheels similar to *racing buggies. Other places buy his buggy wheels, he said with a mix of pride and modesty.*

THEN HE SAID *next week he and his wife were heading to York and they could take me in their buggy. It seemed everyone knew exactly where I was going and for how long I was staying. I thanked him and said I would appreciate going with them to York. Then I couldn't stop smiling because I will be so close to home when I get to York, and I miss everyone so much.*

Then Mr. Wilson told us about how the buggies in different communities were slightly different. Malachi and I both knew that by now and had noticed different colors and different styles during our travels. He said that, just like cars, the buggies were continually improving and slight changes were being made all the time.

When Mr. Wilson finished showing us around, we both thanked him. It was a very nice thing for him to take time off his work and show us so many things. His wife came out with lemonade and sandwiches and we all sat in the shade of a large tree and ate while the two dogs sat watching us, hoping for some tidbits. Mr. and Mrs. Wilson warned me not to feed them, or they wouldn't leave me alone. It was hard to watch the small dogs looking at me with their large brown eyes as I put the food into my mouth.

When we were done, we had a lovely drive back to Leah's house.

I turned to Malachi and was brave. This is what I said, "Are you traveling to different communities because you're looking for a fraa?"

He looked over at me and smiled. "Why would I tell you that? It might be a secret."

"I won't tell anyone. Have you found anybody you like yet?"

He chuckled and I'm sure I saw him blush. Then he looked over at me. "Who said that's what I've been doing?"

"If you don't tell me, I'll have to think that's what you're doing."

"I told you, I'm having a look at different places much like yourself. Are you looking for a husband?"

That made me laugh. "I can tell you that I'm not looking for a husband."

"And I can tell you I'm not looking for a husband either."

I laughed again. I never knew he was so funny, but I never talked to him alone until today. We've always been within a group and when he's been at home, Mamm and Dat were always there.

I never found out why he was traveling around and there was no use asking him again. We talked about home and he made me feel less homesick. He misses his dog, Gruff. I've seen his dog when we had meetings at his parents' house. It's the ugliest dog I've ever seen. Gruff's got orange fur and a lot of it, and one ear is torn. He had Gruff since he was really young and the dog is old now. Malachi told me Gruff wasn't too good the day before he left. He's worried he'll get home to find his dog has died.

It was nice to see a man care so much about his pet dog. As we drove on, we talked a lot more, but I can't remember what we talked about. It wasn't about anything in particular, but he kept making me laugh. If I keep laughing, I'll become like Leah.

I asked him if he was going to Morgantown, as that was my next stop. He told me he was going in the opposite direction. I don't know if he was saying that as a joke, because by then we were back at Leah's house and I couldn't find out. He had James's buggy, so he had to leave me there and then he would come back later for the evening meal.

I helped Leah and her daughters cook. I can't count how many came for dinner tonight. I guess there must've been thirty adults and just as many children. We cooked a large ham, and lots of roasted vegetables and mashed potatoes.

Malachi was one of the last to leave and I hoped he was staying late to talk to me some more. I stayed up late to help the girls clean the kitchen and do the last of the washing up and now I'm so tired I could fall asleep standing up.

So, here I am, staying with the bishop at Morgantown. Mr. and Mrs. Wilson were to bring me to stay with a friend of my mother's, Vida. When we arrived at the house, there were people there and we found out Vida died last night in her sleep. It was quite sad, I thought. Now instead of learning her cooking secrets, I'm going to her funeral soon, and I don't even know her. Mamm will be so sad. Another one of her circle-letter ladies has died. This is the second one this year.

Bishop John, from this community, asked me if I would mind staying with him and his wife until after the funeral, and then he would arrange for me to get to my next place, which will be York. I told him all of that was fine with me.

When I get to York, I'll nearly be home.

The funeral was today, three days after Vida died. She had one son and that's all. He left the community many years ago. No one knew how to contact him. I wrote to Mamm about Vida and I hope the letter gets there before I get home.

The graveyard was on sloping land. It was only a small grave-yard, like the town itself, which I suppose makes perfect sense.

There has been no sign of Malachi and I'm very upset. Perhaps I shouldn't have questioned him so much about why he always turned up at the places where I was. I probably frightened him away. I just wanted to get to know him a little better.

I ARRIVED in York just past sunset. I'm staying with a widow, Ruth Yoder, who has raised ten children. Ten minutes after I arrived there, she told me my mother wants me to know how to run a household. I consider I can do all that now, but I'm still open to learning other things. One thing I know; I can't wait to sleep in my own bed in my own room with Furball again. I'll show everyone at home how good my cooking is and everybody will be surprised. I'd reckon I'd know more than Mamm about cooking some things by now. Especially bread baking, because sometimes her bread doesn't turn out so good. I'd never tell her that, of course, but maybe when I get home she'll let me take over that task. You'd think with all those years of baking it, her bread would be good by now.

I'm really missing Malachi and if I marry him someday, I'll be happy.

HEIDI CLOSED THE DIARY. Her grandmother was falling in love with Malachi and she was reading about it.

That night, Heidi went to sleep with a smile on her face as she thought about what Agnes had said at the beginning of the diary. And that was that she didn't want to fall in love in a mushy way. Now she was heading that way with Malachi, if she was writing about missing him. Heidi was certain that's how Agnes's story was going to end, with her marrying Malachi.

God, please take me back home. I don't want this life. I just want my family back. She closed her eyes, too tired to finish the rest of her grandmother's story and hoping she'd wake up to Derek's soft lips on her forehead telling her he's going to work for the last day before Christmas. She remembered she said she didn't mind if he worked on Christmas Eve. Maybe before her accident they'd arranged to do something else that day. Otherwise, why would she mind?

If she woke up and found herself back home, she and the girls could pretty the house for Christmas. She'd bake more cookies and make that special meal Derek had mentioned to take to his parents for Christmas. Then she decided to use one of her grandmother's recipes as well. She fell asleep hugging Agnes's diary to her chest.

CHAPTER 21

Sunday, December 24

HEIDI WOKE to the sound of her alarm. She sat bolt upright, devastated. She was in her cold and unfriendly apartment. It was a place she'd once loved dearly, but now the white marble and the Italian tiles made it cold and unfriendly compared with her house filled with love, warmth, and joy.

The diary hadn't taken her back. What if she never saw Derek and the children again? Tears streamed down her face.

She stared at the diary lying halfway under the sheet. *Why didn't it work this time?*

Maybe it had been just a coincidence that the two times she'd been reading it she'd crossed from one dimension into the other. Her stomach churned and she blamed herself for leaving Derek all those years ago. And for what? She'd been chasing a stupid whim and then got caught up in money-making greed and pride in her accomplishments.

Now she knew that the most precious things couldn't be bought with money. Everyone always said money couldn't buy happiness, but it had certainly bought her a two-million-dollar apartment. Her apartment was just an object. Yes, it represented all the hard work she'd put in over the years, but she lived in it alone.

Now it wasn't enough for her and she'd gladly give it all away to be back with Derek in their humble home. She felt ashamed that in the past, she'd been too mindful of what others thought of her and that's why she'd never told anyone she'd been Amish.

Before she got out of bed and got back on the treadmill of the everyday familiar routine, she prayed that her life wouldn't always be so wretched.

After she dressed, it was off to the coffee shop for breakfast. Then it would be on to an early appointment before she headed to her office.

Today she had to make some changes. She'd change small things at first. Instead of going home to a lonely TV dinner, she would have dinner out by herself. Wanting to feel close to home, and find out the rest of her grandmother's story, she shoved Agnes's diary into her carry-all bag.

Heidi headed out of her building, relieved that Dennis, the temporary doorman, already had someone talking to him. She slipped out of the building without making eye-contact and walked briskly up the road to the café.

· · ·

As soon as Heidi sat down at her usual booth for breakfast, she thought, *Wouldn't it be fun to change things even further and take a whole year off work?* She could even travel to all the places her grandmother had gone. She trembled when she realized that would mean her business wouldn't grow while she was gone, and might even slide backward. No, she couldn't do it. Then she realized that her business hadn't brought her freedom, it had tied her down.

She pulled the diary out of her bag and as she flipped to the last page, a shiver ran through her. Today was Christmas Eve, and it was Christmas Eve ten years ago to the very day that she left the Amish and left Derek.

Heidi skipped to the last couple of pages and found the last place that her grandmother had visited. It was the place where the widow, Ruth Yoder, was telling her how to keep house.

This is what Ruth said to me this morning, "This is how I ran my day when I had kinner. *Wake up, nurse the* boppli, *cook breakfast for Joseph and enjoy time with him before waking the older* kinner. *Then everyone had breakfast, and then Joseph went to work. I'd wash the dishes and then clean the kitchen. Then I'd make the beds and clean upstairs. Of course, the older* kinner *would help before they went to school. Next, I'd nurse the* boppli *again, put him down for a nap and then clean the living room. Then it would be a meal for the* kinner, *before bed. Then I'd cook the main meal I'd eat with Joseph, then I'd wash the dishes, nurse the* boppli, *give the* boppli *a bath, put him to bed, have a bath myself and then go to bed.*

She tapped a finger on her chin. "I don't think I've left anything out."

"Washing the clothes?" I asked.

"Ah, that's done one day a week, rain or sunshine."

I found it odd she'd tell me how she ran her household, but still, she was only trying to help me. Surely the daily duties would depend on how many children are in the family. No two households would run the same, I'm sure. Maybe Mamm sent me to the place she knew I'd least like before I came home, just so I would miss everyone more. Although she's very nice, I don't feel the connection with Ruth that I've felt with the other women with whom I've stayed.

HEIDI SKIPPED SOME PAGES. If her grandmother didn't enjoy the place, she didn't feel like reading about it. Not today.

I'M HOME NOW and I'm on the last couple of pages of my diary. I've missed seeing Malachi and now I know that I could be interested in marrying him if he feels the same about me. We've never had a conversation about it, so I wouldn't know. We seem to get along well together and I like being with him. He makes me feel good. We have a few people coming for the evening meal tomorrow night and I'm hoping Malachi will be one of them. I've heard he's back. I feel nervous about seeing him again.

My parents were right to send me away. I feel I've grown up into a woman. If they hadn't sent me away, I don't know what would've happened. I've seen all those different communities with different ideas on things. It was good to see how other people lived.

To sum it all up, I've thought about all the people and places I've visited. I've zigzagged across the countryside and met so many nice people. I was sad that Vida from Morgantown died, but I met lovely people at Morgantown and will continue writing to Becky, the daughter of the bishop in the community at Morgantown where I stayed. She's a little younger than I am and we got along really well.

I can close my eyes and say a prayer for everybody, even Sally Anne. I never want to leave home. I'm sure Furball missed me too.

When I walked back into the room for the first time since I went away, he put his head up and looked directly at me. I'm sure his eyes said, 'Don't go away again!' Normally, he just stays asleep whenever I walk into my bedroom.

I hope someday my kinner, *if I have them, and maybe even my* grosskinner *will be interested in my travels and what I've written here.*

I have one page left, so to whoever is reading this, these are my hopes. I hope to be able to live happily on my own, as Elizabeth did, if I ever have to. I hope to be joyful as Leah is, and be able to laugh at everything just as she does.

And, there's one more thing. I will be grateful for every day because we do not know what tomorrow might bring. Tomorrow is not guaranteed; we only have today. We can plan for our future but it is Gott *who decides what will be. We can't know what He has in store.*

TIME WAS GETTING AWAY from her and Heidi closed the book. "I wish I remembered you, *Mammi,*" Heidi whispered as she closed the diary. "More than anything, I want to know if you married Malachi. I don't think you did because my last name is King and if you married Malachi, my last name would be whatever Malachi's last name was. I can't remember what it was, but I know it wasn't King. Oh yes, Arnold, I think it was. That's an unusual name. Hmm. Unless you married twice, but that's not likely."

Maybe she could write to Maize Yoder. Maize was interested in history and kept a lot of the genealogical records of the area where she'd grown up. That way, she would avoid contacting her mother. She just had to know what became of Agnes when Agnes arrived back home.

Then it was back to business for Heidi. Even though it was a Sunday, she had an appointment. Just one, but it was still important. She had a meeting with a realtor to see an office space on the opposite side of the city. Even though she wasn't quite ready to expand the business, if the office space was ideal, she could be tempted to jump in.

As Heidi drained the last of her coffee, she looked at her wristwatch to see she was running late. That would not do. She was always on time for her appointments, and with the traffic the way it was, that wasn't always easy. Heidi slid out of the booth, grabbed her bag and coat, and headed out of the café.

As she stepped onto the sidewalk and looked up the road for a taxi, the rain poured down. Normally she loved the rain, but now it made her miserable. Her business felt like a millstone around her neck rather than a ticket to freedom.

Instead of feeling blue, she told herself, *I should be congratulating myself on how much money I made this year. I can buy anything I want and not worry about budgeting or saving for it.*

As she huddled under the awning of the café to keep out of the rain, she knew she had nothing to look forward to in the new year except more of the same. She wanted to be back with the children and teach them things about life. If she ever crossed back to her other life, she'd be able to tell them all about her grandmother and her travels. She'd also demonstrate all the recipes and all the special hints and tips out of Agnes's book. Now shivering in the cold, she wanted to be back with her family where she belonged.

A cold gust of wind came out of nowhere causing her teeth to chatter. If only she'd worn long pants rather than a skirt. She pulled her warm coat around her and then saw a taxi. It was traveling in the opposite direction, but it suddenly stopped. It was too good an opportunity to miss. With a quick look for traffic, she sprinted across the road. Before she reached the taxi, someone stole it and it had already zoomed away. Not wanting to arrive at her appointment wringing wet, she stepped back under another awning to keep dry. Then it occurred to her she might have put her foldup umbrella in her carryall bag. As she rummaged through her bag, she noticed the diary wasn't there.

I left it in the café.

Looking up at the café now directly across the road, she hoped one of the workers had found the book and put it aside. No longer did she care about her appointment; the diary was more important right now.

As she dashed to get the diary, she heard someone scream, "Stop! Look out!"

Then the sound of screeching brakes rang through the

air and Heidi whipped her head around to see a car heading for her. She froze; it was too late to move. Everything went black.

In the recesses of her fuzzy mind, she heard someone scream about calling 911, but they seemed a million miles away. The next thing she remembered was an image of someone leaning over her in a white coat. There were bright lights behind him. She opened her eyes again and saw a face covered in a mask, and many muffled voices filled the background of her mind.

Was she dying? Was this the end? She didn't want to die, not yet. *I need Derek, I need to see him just one more time. Derek!*

"WAKE UP, Heidi. Wake up. I'm right here."

Heidi opened her eyes when she heard Derek's deep voice. It was he. She had to blink a couple of times because the light was blinding. She looked down at herself and saw she was sitting up in a seat and clutching Agnes's book to herself.

She looked at Derek and watched his mouth open and close as he said, "You'll miss your bus. They're calling it now."

CHAPTER 22

"YOUR BUS IS HERE," Derek repeated when she didn't move.

Heidi straightened up and looked around the bus terminal where she'd left Derek all those years ago. Only thing was, it was happening now. This was it; the moment she'd left Derek, gotten on the bus and ridden right out of his life. This wasn't like the other time she'd been back there. Derek was thinner and boyish. She reached out and touched his smooth shaven face. "Derek, it's you."

"I hope so." His lips twisted with amusement.

If he was young, then that meant … "I'm young again."

He laughed. "I have no idea what you're talking about. Now stand up and put one foot after the other, or you'll miss that bus and you'll blame me for you nodding off."

With one hand to her head, she looked over at the bus bound for New York. The queue was quickly getting shorter as people boarded. Then she looked back at the love of her life.

"What are you waiting for?" He stood and tried to pull her to her feet.

"I'm not going anywhere."

He smiled at her and sat back down. "Do you mean it?"

"*Jah*. I'm staying. I'm never going anywhere again."

He chuckled and hugged her to himself. "I was praying you'd stay and if *Gott* answered my prayers then I told Him I would find the courage to ask you something. Will you marry me, Heidi?"

His words were blurted out and it wasn't even a romantic moment. Heidi's eyes filled with tears when she thought that Agnes would've liked a proposal like that. Now she realized she wasn't only back where she belonged, she was going to get to live out all those precious moments she'd missed, both happy and sad. "I will marry you."

"Do you really mean it?"

She nodded as she willed the tears not to fall. "I do."

"And you're not going to think of leaving—ever?"

"Never again."

He chuckled. "I'm the happiest man in the world. That's the best Christmas gift ever."

As they hugged again, she knew that all the success she'd worked so hard to achieve and all the money in the world paled in comparison to the riches she had with Derek and the community. These were riches that wouldn't fade.

He jumped to his feet, reached over and picked up her bag and swung it over his shoulder, while she held on tight to her grandmother's book.

"Before you take me home, I want to visit *Dat*."

"He's at your place where we just left him."

Heidi laughed, remembering she still lived with her parents. She'd get to spend time with her father all over again. "Good."

As she rode in the buggy next to Derek, he couldn't stop talking and making plans for their future. He worked with his brother, Ben, in a dairy farm and thought he was going to do that forever, but Heidi knew he'd end up doing what he loved for a living.

"Your folks will be so pleased you changed your mind about going."

"*Jah*, they will be." She couldn't wait to see her father again, and see the younger version of her mother.

"You go on ahead and I'll be in soon," Derek said as soon as they arrived.

Heidi jumped down from the buggy and burst into the house. Her parents were in the living room. Her father was reading his Amish newspaper and her mother was eating something. Both had teacups on a low table in front of them, by the backdrop of a crackling fire. "I've decided not to leave."

She stared at her father and wanted to run and hug him, but they never did that in their family.

He simply nodded. "What made you change your mind?"

"I ... I can't say."

Her mother smiled at her. "I'm so happy. I would've worried about you every single day."

"*Nee*, we would've left you in *Gott's* hands, Heidi," her father said.

A knock sounded on the door. "That's Derek. He drove me back. Come in, Derek."

Derek walked in with her bag and Heidi took it from him and pulled out her grandmother's book and handed it back to her father. "It was a very interesting book, *Dat*."

"You read it?"

"All of it. And I read a lot of the recipes."

"And you don't want to keep it?" he asked.

Heidi shook her head. *"Nee."*

He chuckled. "Perhaps you'll want to give it to one of your *kinner* when they're thinking about leaving the community?"

She stared at him open-mouthed. Did he know something about the book?

"You liked it?" her mother asked.

"Nee, I mean, *jah,* it was interesting." She looked back at her father. "I want you to keep it here, *Dat*."

"You're giving it back to me?"

"That's right." Heidi stared at her father and he gave her a knowing smile. She didn't want to risk keeping it in case it had something to do with her travels. Then she remembered she didn't have it with her when she'd been hit by that car. She'd left it at the café.

"What's in that book?" her mother asked looking between the two of them.

"It's a kind of 'travel' book," Heidi's father told his wife.

It was then she wondered if her father had traveled across time somehow too. She looked around her childhood home; it was weird to be back.

"I'll keep the book with me until you want to share it with the *kinner* you'll have some day."

"Who did she marry? Did Agnes marry Malachi, *Dat?*"

He chuckled. "That's a complicated question. My father was Bruno King."

"Oh. What happened to Malachi?"

"Who's Malachi?" her mother asked, looking at her husband.

Heidi said, "A friend of Agnes, and by the way she talked about him I was hoping that they would end up marrying, that's all."

"My *mudder* did marry a man called Malachi Arnold."

"She did?" She stared at her father.

"*Jah.*"

"What happened to him?"

"I'm being confusing. Malachi was my *vadder,* but I don't remember him. He died when I was two, and when I was five, *Mamm* remarried. When I got older, I changed my name to King because he was the only *vadder* I ever knew."

Heidi blinked back tears. "That's so sad. He died?"

"He did."

"She found love again, Heidi," her mother said. It was just like her mother to disregard emotions. They were always hidden in their family.

"You knew all that, *Mamm?*" Heidi asked.

"*Jah,* I just didn't know his name was Malachi. I knew your *vadder's* real *Dat* died."

"I'm so sad. He died so young."

"He went to—"

"A better place, I know, but he didn't get to see his son grow up."

Her mother gasped and Heidi realized her mother thought she shouldn't have said it for some reason. Heidi had always been out of step with her parents. "Sorry, *Dat.*"

"I would like to remember him, but I don't. Bruno King treated me as his own right from the start."

Heidi thought back to Agnes and how she'd gotten to know her well. She was going to say what was on her mind and they'd have to deal with it. "I feel like I know Agnes now from her diary, and I'm just so sad that she married Malachi and then he died."

"There is another diary. More than one, come to think of it," her father said.

That was such good news. "When she got back home, she wrote more?"

"*Jah*, when she married my *vadder*, Malachi."

"She was just falling in love with him when she wrote that diary all about her travels. I'm sad they didn't have a long and happy life together."

"*Jah*, you said that already, more than once," her mother said.

"Tomorrow is guaranteed to none of us, Heidi."

Heidi stared at her father. She was sure she had read something like that in Agnes's diary.

"Remember, it's here for your *kinner* to read one day," *Dat* looked at the diary that now sat atop the low table in front of the couch.

"Speaking of Heidi's future *kinner* ...." Everyone looked at Derek, and then he said, "I have asked Heidi to marry me and she has agreed."

Mrs. King gasped. "Is that why you came back, Heidi?"

"Maybe," Heidi smiled and stared into Derek's eyes.

Derek leaned over and said to Heidi, "I'm going to the bishop's *haus* now and tell him you've agreed to marry me and let's see how fast we can do this."

Heidi nodded. The faster the better, as far as she was concerned.

"I hope that's all right with the both of you," Derek said to Heidi's parents.

"We're happy if Heidi 's happy," her mother said. "I've always wanted a son, and now I'll have one."

He smiled and looked at Mr. King, who hadn't said a word. "Mr. King?"

"You're my *dochder's* choice. I've raised a sensible *maidel.*"

When her father smiled, Heidi knew both of her parents were happy, each in their own way.

"Derek, how about milk and cookies, or some *kaffe?*"

"*Nee, denke,* Mrs. King. I have the bishop to speak with."

Heidi couldn't help the giggle that escaped her lips. After Derek had said goodbye to her parents, she walked him out of the *haus.*

At the front door he turned around, and said, "I'm so happy, Heidi. We'll have a *wunderbaar* life together. I'm going to start looking for a home for us."

She nodded and it was hard to keep from him that they'd buy the old Henderson home and have three beautiful children. There were so many things she wanted to tell him, but first, she'd have to wait and see if things happened the same as when she'd lived them. "There has never been anyone else I've ever considered marrying."

He laughed. "Good to know. And it's the same with me."

"We'll have a happy life together."

"Can I stop by and see you tomorrow?"

"Of course you can. Stay here the whole day if you'd like to."

He gave her a huge grin before he got into his buggy and drove away. She watched the buggy through the half-opened front door until it was a tiny speck in the distance and then until it disappeared altogether.

Even though it seemed she was taking a giant step backward, being back at her parents' again, she headed inside to spend as much time as she could with her father. She might even find out more about Agnes's life.

Heidi's mother was more than a little surprised when she asked if *Mamm* had the ingredients on hand to make *Mammi* Agnes's Christmas cake. Heidi had seen it in the diary somewhere. When she saw it had to be served hot, she decided to make it on Christmas Day, if time permitted.

Agnes's Fruit and Nut Christmas Cake (with date and walnut topping).

Cake Ingredients:

1 1/2 cups dates, finely chopped

1 teaspoon baking soda

1 cup boiling water

1 cup sugar

2 tablespoons butter

2 eggs
1/2 teaspoon baking powder
1 teaspoon cinnamon, optional
1 cup walnut pieces
Flour

Method:
Heat oven to moderate heat, about 350°F
Combine dates and baking soda, then pour boiling water
over the top and let stand.
Combine sugar, butter, eggs, baking powder, cinnamon,
nuts, and enough flour to make a thick mixture.
Pour into a baking dish, place into oven for 40 to 45
minutes.

Topping recipe:
2 cups chopped dates
2 cups chopped walnuts nuts
2 cups water
2 heaped tablespoons flour
coconut for sprinkling just before serving.

Combine first four ingredients in a saucepan over
medium heat
Cook until thick.
Spread over cake while hot.
Sprinkle with coconut while still hot and just before
serving.

CHAPTER 23

December 25

ON CHRISTMAS MORNING, Heidi was delighted she had woken up in her parents' home. When she was enjoying breakfast with her parents, there was a knock on the front door.

"I'll get it." Heidi ran out to the front door hoping it was Derek. She flung it open to see Derek's smiling face and behind him soft snowflakes fell. It was as pretty as a postcard.

"Happy Christmas." Derek handed her a small package.

"Oh, no. I haven't got you anything." They had exchanged small Christmas gifts the day before she'd been due to leave, and she hadn't expected anything else. "I wasn't supposed to be here," she mumbled looking at the parcel.

"I don't need anything. Having you here is my gift. Anyway, this is something I saved. I've had it for a while."

She pulled him inside out of the cold and closed the door. "What is it?"

He placed it into her hands. "It was something I was saving to give you on a very special day. I thought it would be on the day you came back." He chuckled. "But since you didn't leave this is a very special occasion, for me at least."

Heidi could hear her parents talking in the kitchen and was glad they were giving them a quiet moment alone together.

"Open it. Let's sit by the fire," he said.

As they sat in front of the fire, it reminded Heidi of their warm and lovely home—the home they would have one day. She still felt dreadful about not having a gift for him. Slowly, she pulled on the ribbon and untied it, and then she pulled the paper aside to see something familiar. She gasped. It was the white china clock that sat—well, would sit—atop their mantel over their fireplace. If it hadn't been for this clock, Heidi never would've known if the whole thing of traveling between two life-paths had been real or imagined. She found it ironic that a clock, a timepiece, was the object that confirmed that everything about her two alternative futures wasn't just a dream, and that she had traveled back in time to be reunited with Derek.

"Do you like it? I saw it and I knew you'd either love it or hate it. I know you're a practical girl and you don't like little bits and pieces or useless objects around the house."

It was true, that's why she'd had no clutter in her cold unfriendly New York apartment. "It's a clock, though. It's not useless and I love it." Heidi stared at it, not being able to believe it. "It's beautiful. I love it," she repeated.

He smiled and looked a little shocked. "You do? Really?"

"*Jah.* It's beautiful. When we get a *haus* of our own, I'll put it on the mantel right in the middle." She looked into his hazel eyes and saw that he was pleased. This was shaping up to be the best Christmas ever.

Derek left for home then to spend Christmas Day with his family, but first he asked if he could come back around five o'clock and take her to have desserts at his family's home. Her parents said that would be fine.

Heidi helped her mother prepare their Christmas dinner, a small but delightful feast for the three of them. She even had enough time to make Agnes's Christmas cake, and also paid special attention to *Dat,* knowing how much she'd miss him when *Gott* took him home.

When five o'clock came, she was ready and waiting. She said goodbye to *Mamm* and *Dat,* and ran out the door to Derek's buggy. She was a little nervous about how his parents felt now that she'd agreed to marry their son. As if reading her mind, Derek looked over at her and smiled. "Don't worry, Heidi. They're happy you stayed, and happy we're going to get married. I was driving them crazy when I thought you were leaving. And the bishop says we can choose a wedding date in late January. He was good enough to confirm that with me when he stopped by the *haus* early this afternoon."

Heidi gave him a smile at that news, still feeling nervous.

Her worries evaporated when Mrs. Miller greeted her

with a hug, and Mr. Miller gave her a big smile. *Yes*, she thought, *this truly is the best Christmas ever.*

~

Heidi and Derek's wedding day.
January 29

HEIDI WAS DRESSED and brushing out her hair in her bedroom. The wedding was to be held in her parents' house. She felt well prepared for marriage now, thanks to Agnes. She felt as though she'd traveled along with Agnes, and she'd also had the experience of her many lonely years away from the community to make her appreciate home and family that much more. Just as she decided to begin sectioning her hair for braiding, a knock sounded on her door.

"Come in."

Her mother opened the door with something in her hands. "Your *vadder* found something he thought you might like."

"What is it?" She tossed the hairbrush onto the bed and sat down.

Her mother sat down next to her. "These are Agnes's other diaries. Your *vadder* said the dark green one is the one she continued directly after her travels, the black one's when she got married, and the brown one is when she had *Dat*." Her mother absently started braiding one side of her daughter's hair as they talked, so Heidi started in on the other braid.

"I'm so pleased to have these. I can't wait to read them all." She'd read them one at a time and hope that none of them would take her back to New York. She never wanted to go back there. Never would she read them when she was tired or about to fall asleep, just in case.

"He said for you to keep them."

"I will. And also, I think I will get that other one from him because it had so many good recipes."

"I had a little look at these and they have recipes in them too."

"Oh, good." She took her eyes off the diary, and looked at her mother. "I can't believe I'm getting married today."

"Make sure you remember it because it's going to be one of the most important days in your life. The joining together of man and woman in *Gott's* sight is not to be taken lightly."

Heidi nodded. "I know."

"You're old to be getting married. I'm glad you didn't wait longer."

Heidi was just past her twentieth birthday and didn't think she was old to be getting married. For an *Englischer*, it would be very young to be getting married, but to the Amish it was old. She knew she was blessed to find a man like Derek and she didn't see any reason to wait to marry him. She already knew what was out there and there was no one like him.

"I better go down and supervise the food."

"*Denke* for being a good *mudder.*" She gave her mother a hug.

SAMANTHA PRICE

"Don't make me cry," her mother said.

"Don't *you* make me cry."

Her mother gave a little laugh before she walked out the room.

Heidi wasted no time in pinning up her hair. She placed her prayer *kapp* over the top and then sat down and opened the green book to find out exactly what happened when Agnes came back to her community. She didn't have much time, so she'd have to skim across the pages because she couldn't wait to know.

I FIRST SAW *him at the Sunday meeting at the Millers'. He hadn't been to my parents' haus and I hadn't seen him for months. No one talked about where he was and neither did I ask. I just waited and prayed to see him again. We'd traveled in the warm weather and now it was winter. I looked at him and he looked away from me. When the meeting was over, I hurried over to him as soon as I saw he was alone. I asked him how his dog was. He said his dog was fine, just getting slower due to his age. I was so pleased the dog hadn't died. Then I asked why he hadn't been around.*

This is what he said to me, "I went away again to think about everything. Agnes, I had to go home early when you were still visiting. It was a silly thing I was doing following you around the countryside."

"You were following me?"

"I was."

"Why?"

His eyes opened a little wider. "Isn't it obvious?" He smiled at me and I knew what he meant.

234

I smiled back at him and then I was embarrassed by him looking at me and I had to look away.

He leaned closer to me, and whispered, "Your *mudder asked* me to keep an eye on you."

My heart sank like a heavy lead weight, right to the bottom of my feet. "She what?" I was shocked that my mother would involve him like that in my life. She'd really gone too far this time. And she'd upset me. I thought he might have been in love with me.

"It's hard for parents to let go and they have a special place in their hearts for you. They told me they nearly lost you as a *boppli*, and …"

"They shouldn't have sent you all that way to spy on me."

"I wasn't spying. I was checking on you."

I shook my head, angry with my parents.

"Why did you think I kept turning up everywhere?" he asked.

I shrugged my shoulders. I couldn't tell him that I thought he was in love with me. "I kept asking you that."

"You seemed pleased to see me, when you saw me."

"I was. You reminded me of home."

"Is that all?"

I stared into his face. "I don't know what you're talking about."

He chuckled. "Your *mudder* was upset that you were leaving, and I wanted to get to know you more because you never paid me any mind when we were at your parents' house. I thought it was a way to do both; that you and I could get to know each other better and it would make your *Mamm happy* knowing that I'd be there."

I smiled at him. "Your plan worked."

"There is something I must tell you, and that is that I got sick and had to come home early."

"What do you mean you got sick?"

"I won't go into all the details except to say the doctor found out that there is something wrong with me and the plain truth is I don't have long to live."

I could not believe his words. He was the best man I have ever found and now I knew I loved him. I guess that he thought the same because he conspired with my mother to go to all those places at the same time I was at them. He wouldn't have done that if he hadn't liked me. "How bad is your illness?"

"They tell me I don't have long. Six month, maybe more and maybe less."

I held my stomach, I couldn't believe my ears. I felt I was in a bad dream. "We can pray."

"I know where I'm going, Agnes. I will gladly go home with Gott where I belong, at whatever time He wills it."

I couldn't stop the tears that came into my eyes.

"Don't be sad," he told me.

I wanted to scream out that it wasn't fair.

Then he said, "I had plans for us in my mind until I found this out. I guess I shouldn't have built things up until I'd talked to you."

"And have those plans changed now that you have found out about your illness?" We both knew now that we liked each other. No mushy words had to be said.

"I don't want to be a burden on you, Heidi."

"Wouldn't that be my choice to make, if I want to take on that burden?"

He shook his head. "I wouldn't put you in that position."

"Would you deny me what we could have in however long a time you have left?"

He smiled. "I didn't think of it in that way."

"You should start thinking that way." I was trying to find

words to tell him that I liked him without saying them, I just wanted him to know that I didn't care how long we had.

"I had planned at the end of your trip to ask if you would marry me."

"You were?"

He smiled and his eyes twinkled. "That's right."

"And if I tell you I'm willing to accept any time Gott gives us together, what would you say about that?"

"I wouldn't say anything about that."

I looked down quite sad because I wanted him to ask me to marry him.

Then he said, "I wouldn't say anything, but I would ask you this; Agnes, would you marry me?"

He was still being funny even in an important moment like this. I liked his joyful heart. "Jah, I will."

My words pleased him and I wanted more than anything to spend the rest of our lives making him happy. His happiness meant more to me than my own. "Now tell me what illness you have."

"I have cancer."

I'd heard of it and I knew it was bad. I told him we would face it together.

"IT'S TIME, HEIDI," her mother opened the door and saw her reading. "You can't be doing that now. Everyone is waiting for you downstairs. And look at you, you're crying."

"It's sad, you see he's dying." Heidi wiped away a tear. "And it's also happy because they're getting married."

"Who?"

"My grossdaddi, and grossmammi. Agnes and Malachi."

She shook her head. "Put the book down now and wipe your eyes, and then find your smile and come downstairs and get married."

Heidi wiped her eyes once more, and placed the book back down on top of the other two. She couldn't wait to read more, but it might have to wait until she got back from the one week's vacation of visiting relatives that Derek had planned.

Heidi looked out the window. "More people are coming. Do you think we should wait for them to get inside the *haus?*"

Mamm leaned across Heidi and looked out the window. "Just another few minutes until you have dried your eyes then."

"*Denke, Mamm.*"

As soon as her mother shut the door, she couldn't wait any longer. She quickly grabbed another diary and leafed through it.

I saw the doctor for the first time with Malachi and found out more about what was wrong with him. The doctor explained it to me and didn't give us false hope, which I appreciated. The doctor didn't see any reason why we couldn't get married and he said there's no reason why Malachi can't father children. It was one of my main concerns, and Malachi's. Once we found that out, there was no reason to delay our nuptials.

Malachi suggested we get married at the end of the month on January 29, if I still wanted to marry him. So that is the date our wedding is to be.

. . .

HEIDI FROZE. That was today's date. How uncanny for it to be the exact date as her wedding and not only that, but also to be reading about it on that very date. She scanned down the page to find where she was up to.

We are getting married with the knowledge that we may not have a long time, but that we would certainly make it a good time.

HEIDI HEARD the crowd talking downstairs and she closed the diary. What a good attitude her grandparents had. She was so pleased to be able to call them her grandparents, and so blessed to know both of them through her grandmother's writing. Malachi was a good man, quiet with a sense of humor. Agnes was a strong-willed, determined and adventurous woman with a touch of an entrepreneur's spirit, just like herself.

NOW, she focused on her wedding. Just like her grandmother, she would make the most of each day because it was a gift. She looked down at her clothes to make sure everything looked good and she hadn't forgotten anything. The blue dress she and her mother had sewed together and finished with a week to spare looked perfect. They had also worked together on sewing her white cape, apron, and *kapp*.

She looked down at her black leather lace-up boots and gave a little giggle as she remembered that not so long ago she wouldn't be caught dead in anything but stilettos.

She took a deep breath, and then opened the door.

Her mother's smiling face was the first thing she saw.

Her mother then nodded toward the stairs. "Everyone's waiting."

Heidi walked down the stairs with her mother close behind her. As her foot hit each step, she thought about the real estate business that she'd allowed to take over her life. No longer would she be burdened by staff problems or worried about leads, systems, or expansion. And that's just how she wanted things because a huge weight had been lifted off her shoulders.

Derek was at the bottom of the stairs and he looked up and stared at her as a hush fell across everyone in the house.

Soon they were both standing before the bishop as a married couple. Heidi and Derek signed the necessary paperwork, accompanied by the rich tones of Zachariah Yoder's voice singing a hymn, and then they headed outside to the undercover area by the barn for the wedding breakfast.

This was the start of their life together and, unlike Agnes, she was marrying a man who was healthy. She couldn't imagine how it would've been for her grandmother. Still, Heidi was determined to take heed of the lessons she'd learned and take nothing for granted. No one is promised tomorrow.

Heidi had shared with her mother some of the recipes from Agnes's diary and they made them for the wedding. They had the sauerbraten and several of Agnes's favorite lemon meringue pies were on the desserts table.

It had taken Heidi a while to adjust to being back in the community and, although she still had many questions that had never been satisfactorily answered, she knew her life was better in the community than out.

ELEVEN MONTHS LATER, Heidi and Derek spent their first Christmas together in the home they had bought and renovated. It had come as no surprise to Heidi when Derek suggested they buy the old Henderson home by the mill. The home had the lovely stone fireplace she remembered, and on moving-in day, Heidi placed the special clock that Derek had given her right in the center of the mantel.

A FEW MONTHS into Derek and Heidi's second year together, Heidi had a dream.

She was strolling through the markets, just looking at one thing and another. A woman she didn't recognize approached her, stopping right in her path. Heidi stopped, puzzled. The woman smiled and handed Heidi a bag of oranges, saying, "Here. These are for your baby girl, a gift from her great grandmother."

Heidi woke with a start. She realized Derek was just waking, too, so she got up to start her day.

After breakfast, she asked Derek if she could use the buggy to visit her parents. He said, "Okay, as long as you take me to work first." So Heidi headed to her parents house as soon as she'd delivered Derek.

After greetings had been exchanged, her mother went back to making bread in the kitchen and Heidi sat with *Dat* in the living room. She told her father about her dream. As she described the woman, his eyebrows rose.

He could see the question written on her face. He said, "Yes, Heidi, you're describing my mother, your *Mammi* Agnes."

About nine months after the dream, Heidi gave birth to a baby girl, and Derek asked if they could name her Molly. Heidi agreed happily, telling him she liked that name too.

A year after that, their daughter Jessica was born. Heidi's father died when Jessica was a baby, and everything else unfolded just as Heidi had experienced. Derek's brother, Ben, married her friend, Faith, and they opened the Amish crafts store, and Derek's woodworking hobby soon became his full time job.

Heidi got to experience each of the moments that were important in her life. Even Michael came along just as she had suspected he would. Heidi fell down the rain-slicked porch steps chasing after her girls when Michael was a few months old; she had a memory lapse and a slight concussion. She soon recovered, grateful that there were no lingering problems.

Heidi never went back to her old life in New York City and neither did she miss it.

Every day, Heidi thanked God for her life with Derek and their children here in the Amish community, and she was grateful that, the second time around, she never got on that bus. It had been a blessing to know her grandmother through her diary and have the advantage of the life lessons of someone older and wiser. She always treasured the gift of that dream-glimpse of her grandmother Agnes.

Heidi often wondered how many others had the

chance to see where their life choices would take them. How many people got to turn back the clock? She was glad that she'd been given another chance all those years ago, and thankful her travels had brought her home to Derek all those years ago in time for an Amish Christmas.

Merry Christmas

Thank you for reading In Time for an Amish Christmas.

www.SamanthaPriceAuthor.com

THE NEXT BOOK IN THE SERIES

Are you ready for another stand-alone Christmas novel?
Book 2:
Amish Christmas Bride.

Many said Matt Yoder was the most handsome Amish bachelor in the county, maybe even the country. When he contacted Jane and asked her to return to the community where she grew up, she was convinced all her prayers had been answered. She'd always dreamed of marrying Matt and having a large family.

Her dream turned into a nightmare when she discovered the real reason he wanted her there. He was tired of being single and declared he would be married by Christmas. He had narrowed his search to five women and was having trouble deciding between them.

Since Matt had always overlooked Jane, was it already too late?

Or can she find a way to make him see that she is and always has been his perfect Amish match?

RECIPES FROM THE BOOK

From Chapter 2.
Mammi's Chicken and Onion stew.
Ingredients
2-4 tablespoons of cooking oil or fat
1 whole chicken (about 5#) cut into pieces
1-2 pounds onions, thin-sliced
1 pound carrots, sliced or chopped
1 pound peas-in-pods, whole or halved
2-5 cloves of garlic, minced
salt and pepper to taste
Herbs as desired (sage, thyme, rosemary, marjoram ...)
Chives or parsley for garnish, snipped

Cookware:
Large soup pot
Large frying pan

Method:

In frying pan, brown chicken pieces in 2 tablespoons
of oil.

Transfer to soup pot and cover with water, rinsing juices
from frying pan into soup pot. Cover the pot.

Bring to a boil, then simmer for 1 to 2 hours. (If desired,
debone the chicken at this point, and return meat to soup
pot) continue to simmer.

In frying pan, brown sliced onions in 1 – 2 tablespoons of
oil or fat. Then add 1 cup water and stir. Add onions and
broth to the soup pot, and continue to simmer.

Add carrots, garlic, and choice of herbs, and simmer until
carrots are tender.

Add peapods, simmer 10 – 20 min.

Salt and pepper to taste.

Thicken with flour or roux.

*Add water as needed during cooking time to make
desired amount of gravy.

*Serve with boiled red-skin potatoes or with mashed
potatoes.

*Makes a good soup, too, with added liquid and
seasonings to make more broth, and any other added
vegetables you choose.

Pork Casserole with Sauerkraut
Ingredients:
5 pounds pork ribs with meat
1 pound onions, sliced thin

2 – 4 quarts sauerkraut, amount based on your
preferences
1-2 tablespoons black peppercorns
2 tablespoons cooking oil or fat
Cookware:
1 or 2 large and deep casserole dishes with lids
Large frying pan
Method:
Heat oven to 375° F
In frying pan, brown onions in cooking oil or fat.
Layer in bottom of casserole dish (dishes) including liquid
from pan.
Place ribs in a layer over onions.
Sprinkle with peppercorns.
Spread sauerkraut over top of meat, adding juice as well.
Add 1 – 2 cups water, then cover with lid.
Bake in hot oven (375° F) for 1 – 2 hours, until bubbling
around sides of casserole dish.
Lower oven temperature to 250° F and bake for several
more hours.
Add water if needed to prevent drying out.
Done when meat is 'fall-apart-tender.'
Usually does not need added salt, but put some on the
table for individual use.

Serve with mashed potatoes and garden vegetables of choice.

From Chapter 7.

Cookies.

Ingredients.

8 ounces of butter

1 1/4 cups of icing sugar or confectioners' sugar

2 teaspoons of vanilla extract

2 cups of plain flour

1/2 cup of rice flour and

1/3 cup of cornflour (cornstarch)

2 tablespoons full of milk

Method:

Beat butter, sifted icing sugar and extract in large bowl until pale and fluffy. Stir in combined sifted flours into batches then add milk until mixed well.

Divide mixture into half.

Knead each half on a floured surface until smooth. Shape each half into a ball and keep them loosely covered in a cool place until firm, about an hour.

Preheat oven to medium heat.

Grease the oven trays.

Roll out one ball of dough until ¼ inch thick.

Cut shapes as desired with cookie cutters.

Place on trays one inch apart.

Repeat this process with the second ball of dough.

Collect dough scraps, shape into a ball, roll out and cut out more cookies.

Bake cookies for 8-12 minutes or until golden brown. Stand on trays for 5 minutes before removing from the oven tray to a tea towel or paper for further cooling. Store in a tightly-sealed container.

~

Peach cake

1 cup flour

1 teaspoon baking powder

2 tablespoons of butter

1 teaspoon of sugar

1/3 of a teaspoon of salt

eight canned or fresh peach halves, reserving juice if using canned peaches

1/4 cup of sugar

1/2 teaspoon of cinnamon

one egg

1/2 cup of milk

reserved peach syrup

Method:

Rub butter into flour, baking powder, salt, and sugar to make fine crumbs.

Press this mixture into a greased round dish, 8 inches in diameter.

Cover with drained peach halves, flat sides down and round sides up.

Sprinkle with combined sugar and cinnamon.

Cook in a moderate oven for 15 minutes.

Take out of the oven

Beat egg and milk until well blended.

Spoon gently over the peach halves.

Return to oven and cook for 30 minutes.

Use the reserved syrup and serve the cake with the syrup as the sauce. To do so, heat the syrup in a saucepan and thicken with 1 tablespoon of cornstarch stirred into 1/4 cup cold water.

From Chapter 13.

Family Beef and Potato Pie

Ingredients:

3 pounds ground beef

1 large onion, chopped

¼ cup flour

2-3 cups beef broth or water

1 pound cheese, grated

5 pounds potatoes, boiled and mashed in advance

salt and pepper to taste

optional – peas, corn, lightly cooked chopped carrots,
about 2 pounds total.

Cookware

Large frying pan

Large deep casserole dish

Method

Heat oven to 325 F

Brown beef and onion in frying pan, adding salt and
pepper if desired.

Stir flour into juices in frying pan, mixing until smooth.

Add broth or water slowly, stirring constantly to make a
thick gravy.

Layer into casserole as follows:

1/3 of the meat mixture

½ of vegetables (if using them)

½ of cheese

¼ of mashed potatoes

Repeat above layers, then all remaining meat.

Remaining mashed potatoes as top crust, covering to edges of the dish.
Bake until bubbling-hot throughout and top of mashed potatoes is browned. (About 1 hour).

Lemon Meringue Pie

First you'll need to bake the pastry.
Sweet Pie Cookie-style Pastry:
Ingredients:
½ cup butter
½ cup sugar
2 cups flour
1 egg

Method:
Cream the butter and the sugar.
Add egg and beat well
Add sifted flour.
Knead lightly
Roll out to size and press into pie tin.
Bake in a moderate oven for about twenty minutes, until lightly browned.
Set on a rack to cool.

Filling:
Ingredients:
2 tablespoons of plain flour
2 tablespoons of cornflour (cornstarch)
Half a cup of white sugar

Half a cup of lemon juice
Half a cup of boiling water
Two egg yolks
Grated outer-layer of one lemon (the "zest")
1 tablespoon butter

Meringue:
2 egg whites
4 tablespoons of sugar

Method:
Blend flour, cornflour and sugar in a saucepan with water along with the lemon juice. Bring to a boil while stirring constantly.
Boil until it thickens and keep stirring.
Add lightly- beaten egg yolks, butter and lemon rind, and stir until mixed well.
Place in already baked and cooled pie crust.

Beat egg whites until stiff
Add sugar gradually and continue beating until thick.
Pile on top of pie and place in a very moderate oven or under a slow griller until lightly brown.

Crushed-cookie Pie Crust
Ingredients:
2 cups crushed cookies
½ cup melted butter
⅓ cup sugar

Method:

Mix all the ingredients together and press evenly onto the base and sides of the pie dish

Bake in a moderately high oven for ten minutes.

From Chapter 17.

Doughnuts: (Makes around fifteen)

Ingredients:

Half a pound of flour

2 teaspoons of baking powder

One pinch of salt

One pinch of nutmeg

4 tablespoons of butter

¼ cup of sugar

Two eggs

Half a cup of milk

Caster sugar (also called superfine sugar)

One lemon

Method:

Sift together: flour, baking powder, salt, and nutmeg.

Rub in butter, add sugar, then well beaten eggs, and sufficient milk to mix into a soft dough.

Turn onto a floured board

Roll out a cord half an inch thick

Cut into rings with the doughnut cutter.

Fry until doughnuts are golden brown.

Sprinkle with caster sugar and serve hot with slices of lemon.

≈

From Chapter 22.

Agnes's Fruit and Nut Christmas Cake (with date and walnut topping).
Cake Ingredients:
1 1/2 cups dates, finely chopped
1 teaspoon baking soda
1 cup boiling water
1 cup sugar
2 tablespoons butter
2 eggs
1/2 teaspoon baking powder
1 teaspoon cinnamon, optional
1 cup walnut pieces
Flour

Method:
Heat oven to moderate heat, about 350°F
Combine dates and baking soda, then pour boiling water over the top and let stand.
Combine sugar, butter, eggs, baking powder, cinnamon, nuts, and enough flour to make a thick mixture.
Pour into a baking dish, place into oven for 40 to 45 minutes.

Topping recipe:
2 cups chopped dates
2 cups chopped walnuts nuts
2 cups water

2 heaped tablespoons flour
coconut for sprinkling just before serving.

Combine first four ingredients in a saucepan over
medium heat
Cook until thick.
Spread over cake while hot.
Sprinkle with coconut while still hot and just before
serving.

AMISH CHRISTMAS BOOKS

In Time for an Amish Christmas

Amish Christmas Bride

Amish Bachelor's Christmas

A Blessed Amish Christmas

ALL SAMANTHA PRICE'S SERIES

Amish Maids Trilogy
A 3 book Amish romance series of novels featuring 5 friends finding love.

Amish Love Blooms
A 6 book Amish romance series of novels about four sisters and their cousins.

Amish Misfits
A series of 7 stand-alone books about people who have never fitted in.

The Amish Bonnet Sisters
To date there are 28 books in this continuing family saga. My most popular and best-selling series.

Amish Women of Pleasant Valley
An 8 book Amish romance series with the same characters. This has been one of my most popular series.

Ettie Smith Amish Mysteries
An ongoing cozy mystery series with octogenarian sleuths. Popular with lovers of mysteries such as Miss Marple or Murder She Wrote.

Amish Secret Widows' Society
A ten novella mystery/romance series - a prequel to the Ettie Smith Amish Mysteries.

Expectant Amish Widows
A stand-alone Amish romance series of 19 books.

Seven Amish Bachelors
A 7 book Amish Romance series following the Fuller brothers' journey to finding love.

Amish Foster Girls
A 4 book Amish romance series with the same characters who have been fostered to an Amish family.

Amish Brides
An Amish historical romance. 5 book series with the same characters who have arrived in America to start their new life.

Amish Romance Secrets
The first series I ever wrote. 6 novellas following the same characters.

Amish Christmas Books

Each year I write an Amish Christmas stand-alone romance novel.

Amish Twin Hearts
A 4 book Amish Romance featuring twins and their friends.

Amish Wedding Season
The second series I wrote. It has the same characters throughout the 5 books.

Amish Baby Collection
Sweet Amish Romance series of 6 stand-alone novellas.

Gretel Koch Jewel Thief
A clean 5 book suspense/mystery series about a jewel thief who has agreed to consult with the FBI.

Made in the USA
Middletown, DE
17 November 2024